THE PROMISE

THE PROMISE

by

Sallie Lee Bell

ZONDERVAN PUBLISHING HOUSE
GRAND RAPIDS, MICHIGAN

PRINTED IN THE UNITED STATES OF AMERICA

THE PROMISE

Chapter One

Ted and Tag were twins, but no one would have believed it by just looking at them. Ted was taller and much stronger, even when only a baby. He was dark, with deep black eyes and a mop of unruly black hair, while Tag had fair skin like his mother, blue eyes and waving blond hair. People took Tag for a girl when he was quite small, until his father insisted that he have his hair cut short, so that there would be no mistake about his being a boy.

Of course their names were not Ted and Tag, but when they were still quite small, their father, Theodore Sharp, had jokingly given them the nicknames which had immediately stuck with them. Ted was named for his father and Tag was named for his grandfather, but neither of the small twins actually knew their real names. When visitors asked them their names, each would repeat the nickname with which their father had dubbed them.

Ted was more aggressive. Even when he was just learning to walk, he was constantly searching for some new adventure. His mother was kept on the alert watching him, for fear that he would hurt himself while toddling about their small home. While he tottered around on his unsteady legs, Tag, who was not only smaller but was two hours younger, would be following him as well as he could on his still more unsteady little legs.

Grace and Theodore were scarcely twenty when the twins were born. They had been sweethearts from their early school days in the little village in South Louisiana.

7

They lived in a trailer on the edge of town and were having a struggle to make their scant wages hold out. When they were first married, Theodore had been injured in an accident at the plant in a nearby town where he was employed. Before he was able to get back to work, the young couple had used up the little compensation that the company had allowed for his accident.

But they were ecstatically happy when they knew that they were to become parents, for, with the optimism of youth, they were sure that they would get along somehow. Both of them had lost their parents when they were in their early teens and they had lived with friends until they were old enough to be married and be on their own.

The twins were happy in their ignorance of the poverty of their parents and the small trailer which was their home was as comfortable to them as if it had been a mansion.

When they were three, they began to try to play games that they saw older boys playing on the vacant lot nearby. Some of these games were too rough for such youngsters, but, with the daring and aggressiveness of Ted, they tried to imitate the older boys. Sometimes they were partly successful, and sometimes their games had disastrous results.

Once they had tried a wrestling game that they had seen when two boys were fighting because of an argument they had started. It looked like fun to Ted, so he suggested that they should try that game also. As usual, Tag was willing to do anything that Ted suggested, but in the tussle Tag fell and sprained his ankle so that he could not walk for several days.

Not long after this, when he had recovered and his injury was forgotten, they saw another game which was more interesting than anything they had seen before. Two boys were fencing, using long pointed sticks for swords. The two parried and thrust while the others cheered the contestants.

Finally the game ended and the boys left the lot and their swords behind them. As soon as they had left, Ted decided that it would be fun for them to have a try at that exciting game and, as usual, Tag agreed that it would be. They slipped over to the lot, disobeying their mother's warning never to leave their own small fenced lot in the trailer court. There was danger outside the trailer court, but the children weren't aware of that and they had disobeyed their mother on a previous occasion:

There were only a few small trees in the trailer court, while just across the road was the bayou whose sluggish waters made their leisurely way downstream. Along the banks of the bayou there was tempting shade below the ancient oaks with their gnarled branches dipping down into the water. And those hyacinths, with their bright green leaves like wax and the petals that seemed to reflect the blue of the sky, with the dot of gold within their hearts, were so temptingly beautiful. They couldn't resist the temptation to get some of them. Ted led the way as usual and he was the one who reached out first to try to pluck one of the blooms. His foot slipped and down he went into the water. Fortunately it wasn't deep near the bank and he managed to catch hold of a small tree trunk hanging over the water and, with the help of Tag, he reached safety, but went home dripping wet.

The punishment they received made them remember to be obedient until now, but the sight of those two wooden swords was too much for Ted. He slipped through the gate, ran into the lot and retrieved the swords, then raced back with them, hoping that his mother had not seen him. When he returned triumphantly with the swords, he immediately gave Tag instructions on how to play the game. They posed as they had seen the older boys do and then each made a lunge at the other. They missed and drew apart, then lunged again after they had regained their weapons which they had dropped. This time Tag was quicker with his stroke than Ted. He had tried to do as the older boy had done, aim at his opponent's

heart, but as he lunged, Ted intercepted the blade and
deflected the aim, but did not stop its speed. The sharp
wooden point plunged into Ted's neck. There was a spout
of blood from the jagged wound and Ted fell down
screaming with pain. Tag stood near echoing Ted's
screams, frightened and guilty.

At the sound their mother looked out, saw the blood
and ran to Ted with a cry of fright. One of the neighbors
who had seen what had happened and who had children
of her own, came to the rescue. She lifted Ted in her arms
and ran with him to her trailer nearby, meanwhile assuring
Grace that the child wasn't seriously injured, in spite of
the spurt of blood which had already begun to coagulate.

She sterilized the wound, put an astringent lotion on
it and covered it with gauze and adhesive tape.

"I don't think he'll have any more trouble, so don't
worry about it," she advised as Grace stood there help-
less, with tears in her eyes.

"Then you don't think I need to take him to a doctor?"
she asked, wondering how she could pay the bill.

"No, I'm sure you don't need to do that," the friend
assured her. "That wasn't such a deep cut as all that.
You just let that bandage stay there until tomorrow and if
you'll bring him over, I'll put a new one on. I've seen
lots worse cuts than that with my four kids and they got
along all right. We'll see how it looks tomorrow, but I'm
sure you'll see that it won't amount to much."

Grace thanked her and said she'd bring Ted back. Ted
had stopped crying as soon as the neighbor began to
dress the wound, but Tag stood by, whimpering. He was
afraid that he had killed Ted and hadn't recovered from
the shock.

Just as the kind neighbor had predicted, the wound was
not serious and it was soon healed, but it left an ugly
jagged scar. His mother grieved about it, but Ted was
rather proud of it, for he had received much attention
because of it. Tag hovered over him, trying to atone for
what he had done. Ted showed his scar to the small

children living in a trailer nearby and swelled with pride as they exclaimed over it and he explained that he had been wounded by a sword.

Life moved happily along for them in their little home, but their parents began to worry over their situation and wondered what they would be able to do when the boys were old enough to start school. The others who lived in the court all had cars, such as they were, and they took their children into town to school, but the Sharps couldn't afford a car. Theodore had to walk a long distance to the bus stop when he went in to work. But, with their usual hopefulness, they decided that there was no use worrying about the future. They would enjoy each day as it came, happy in their love for each other and their two boys. They would let the future take care of itself. There surely must be better days ahead.

Their hopes were never realized, for before the end of the year, both of them were gone and two little boys were left alone with no near relative and no one to take care of them.

Theodore had been taken to the hospital with a sudden attack of appendicitus and he died a few days later from an infection when the appendix ruptured.

When Grace was on her way to the bus stop as she was going to the hospital to be with Theodore, not knowing that he was already dead, she was hit by a drunken driver on the highway and killed instantly.

They were both buried in the little cemetery near the small town while two small boys looked on in frightened wonderment, scarcely understanding what had happened.

The kind neighbor who had dressed Ted's wound took care of them for a short time, but she couldn't keep them. She and her husband were poor and their family was already crowding the trailer. For two or three nights she slept with the children in their own trailer, then, in desperation, she went to the pastor of the church which she attended. He had already learned of the plight of the twins and when she came to him he told her that there were two couples who would each be willing to take one of the boys and keep them until some relative might be located.

The kind neighbor was much relieved and the boys were left with the pastor until he could contact the two couples who had agreed to take the boys.

For the first time in their short lives, the little boys were separated. They were so bewildered and frightened that they had scarcely uttered a word since their tragedy, except when compelled to answer questions.

They were too frightened even to cry during the whole time, but when Tag saw Ted helped into a car while his foster parents drove away with him, he let out a heart-despairing wail.

"I want my brother!" he cried. "I want my Ted! I want my Mommy! I want my Daddy! I want my brother!"

His foster parents, Mr. and Mrs. James, tried to comfort him with soothing words, but they failed in their attempt, for he still kept wailing. He struggled against them when one of them lifted him and put him in the car. He tried to get out and almost fell before Mrs. James could get in and sit beside him.

"Don't cry, little one," she whispered soothingly. "We're going to be your own mother and daddy and we're going to try to make you very, very happy. You'll have lots of toys and playthings and you'll have a nice home to live in and a nice yard to play in. Don't cry. We'll love you heaps."

"But I want my brother. I want my home and I want my Mommy and Daddy. What for did they put 'em in those big boxes and put 'em into the ground?"

"Because they went to heaven, dear," she told him tenderly.

"I want to go there, too, but I don't want to be put in a big box," he wailed.

He had never heard of heaven, but if that was where

his Mommy and Daddy were, there was where he wanted to go. Then he remembered Ted again.

"I want my brother. Where did they took him?" he asked and looked at this stranger with tear-filled eyes.

"They took him to a nice big house where he'll be happy," Mrs. James said, feeling inadequate to cope with this terribly heart-broken little boy and this trying situation.

Her heart ached for the child, for she loved him already. She felt even now that he already belonged to her, though she had no legal right to him.

"I want him! I want him!" he wailed. "I can't play without him. I can't!" and he sobbed with great tearing sobs.

She knew that she would have a hard time trying to make him happy, but she was determined to try at least.

As they drove to their home, she wondered how long it would take this child to forget the horror of what had happened to him and how long it would be before he would accept her as his mother. He was so young that she hoped that through her love and her prayers, he would learn to love her as she already loved him. Only the future would tell. She trusted in the One who held the future in His hands.

Agnes and Richard James had never had any children, though they had wanted children for many years. When they had the opportunity to take care of Tag, they both thought that it was the leading of the Lord and Agnes prayed from the very first moment, that they could keep the child and that he would become reconciled to having them for his parents. She hoped that in time he would forget his brother, for if he couldn't do that, he would always be unhappy over being separated from him.

The first weeks were difficult ones for her. The very first night, after she had given Tag his supper and put him into bed and given him a goodnight kiss, he had slipped out of bed, struggled into his clothes and slipped from the house.

When she came into the room the next morning, the bed was empty. She was terrified and as soon as she and her husband hurriedly talked it over, he phoned the police. After a long and agonizing search that day, there was no sign of Tag and they had almost given up hope of finding him. Agnes was sure that someone must have picked him up and carried him away. She could think of terrifying things that could have happened to him.

Finally as dark was approaching, one of the searchers came upon a very tired little boy lying beside a sideroad, fast asleep under some bushes. They had almost passed him when one of the men saw a little shoe sticking out of the bushes. Agnes was sure that Tag was dead, but when they led her to him lying there unconscious of whatever danger might threaten him, she uttered a glad cry of thanksgiving that he was still alive.

Tag woke at the sound and sat up, blinking in the light of the large flashlight. Agnes took him in her arms and held him to her for a moment without saying a word, while tears coursed down her cheeks.

"Why did you run away, darling?" she asked finally. "Don't you love us just a little when you know we love you so much? Why did you leave us?"

"I wanted to find my brother," he said in a weak quavering little voice. "I miss him. I can't play without him."

"If you'll come home with me and not run away any more and promise to try to let us make you happy, I'll promise that some day, you'll be with your brother again."

She wondered if she had been wise in making this promise and she wondered how she could keep it, but she was determined to try.

"When'll you do that?" he asked skeptically. "Tomorrow?"

"Maybe not tomorrow," she said, "but as soon as we can find him."

"Okay." he agreed with a sigh and soon he was fast asleep again.

Chapter Two

The first thing that Tag asked his foster mother when he wakened the next morning was, "Am I gonna find my brother today?"

"Remember, I said not today," she replied, "for you have to rest. You're a very tired little boy and I want you to be able to play with your brother when you two get together again."

Her heart was heavy, for she was afraid that if the two children met again, it would be still more difficult for the child to adjust to life separated from him. She thought that, perhaps, if she kept putting him off, he might forget in time and her problem would be settled about that, at least.

True to her plan, she kept putting him off with one excuse after another, but when she noticed how his big blue eyes clouded and how his lower lip trembled while he tried to keep from crying, her conscience pricked her. It pricked her still more, when, a week or so later, after the little runaway had been found and she gave him the same answer, he looked at her accusingly and said, "But you promised me a long time ago."

She couldn't put him off any longer, so she decided to take him to see his brother, no matter what the consequences might be.

When they started out in the car, Tag was so excited that he couldn't keep still, but kept jumping up and down on the back seat. When they reached the trailer court, there was no sign of the trailer. She wondered if the child would remember. He did.

As they stopped, wondering what to do and finally decided to go on to the pastor's home, Tag exclaimed,

"What happened? There ain't no more home. What did they do with it?" and he began to cry.

"Don't cry, darling," Agnes begged. "Your brother wouldn't be there. We'll find him."

When they reached the minister's home and Agnes told him why they had come, he shook his head and his eyes rested upon the eager little boy with deep pity in them.

"I'm afraid he's going to be disappointed," he told her. "Just two days after you left, the couple who took the other boy left here. I think the husband got a promotion in his work and was transferred to some other place. I didn't know them very well, for they hadn't been here long and they did not attend church too often. I suppose I should have done something about the boy, but everything happened so fast and they had such good recommendations from those who knew them, that I did not take time to investigate about possible relatives. I was away on my circuit when they left. I'm sorry that the little fellow will be disappointed."

"Perhaps it was all for the best," Agnes sighed. "I've prayed about this and I know that God makes no mistakes, but I don't know what to tell Tag."

"Where is my brother?" Tag piped up from the back seat. "You promised I would find him today."

Agnes went back to the car and opened the door.

"Come up here, darling, and I'll tell you all about it," she told him.

Tag obediently climbed to the front seat and she took him upon her lap as they drove away.

"Ted isn't here," she said as he looked into her eyes questioningly and doubtfully. "His new Mommy and Daddy went away and they took Ted with them. Now we'll have to wait until we can go to see him in his new home. I'm sorry, honey, terribly sorry, but I did the best I could."

His big eyes filled with tears which overflowed and ran down his ruddy little cheeks, while sobs shook him.

"I want Ted! I want my brother!" he sobbed while she held him close and let him cry until finally the sobs ceased and he remained quiet in her arms. She couldn't say anything that would comfort him, so she just let him cry.

"How would you like a cute little dog to play with?" Richard asked after the sobs had ceased.

"I'd like it a lot!" Tag exclaimed, forgetting his grief for the moment.

"Then we'll go and get you one right away," he promised as he gave his wife a smile of encouragement.

They drove to a friend's home where Richard knew that they had several puppies for sale.

The little fellow was entranced when arrangements had been made for him to have the puppy, a little silky-haired cocker spaniel, just old enough to be weaned from its mother.

He petted the little dog and hugged it affectionately. Agnes was pleased to see how carefully he handled the puppy. She had been afraid that, with the natural cruelty that many children have with animals, he would hurt the dog until she could make him understand how to handle it. But when she saw how tenderly he carressed it, while he let it lick his face, she knew that she need have no fear about the dog's safety.

Agnes knew that, though the child was not legally adopted and perhaps never would be unless they could be sure that no relative would appear to claim him, she had a responsibility to teach him something that she feared he had never known. She was sure that his parents had never taught him a thing about God and she knew that, young as he was, that was the most important part of his education. She began by teaching him a simple child's prayer that she knew he could remember. At bedtime she knelt beside him and told him that they would talk to God and then she repeated the simple words and had him repeat them after her. She knew that questions would follow and she was not mistaken.

"What for did we do that?" he asked.

"Because we must talk to God so that He will help us know how to live right," she explained, knowing full well that this didn't enlighten him. She marveled at his ignorance, but welcomed this opportunity to begin to impart to him the same knowledge that she would have imparted to her own little boy, if she had been blessed with one. She looked upon this child as the answer to her prayers for the child God had never given her. It was best this way, she was certain, or it would never have happened.

"Who is God?" he asked.

"God is Someone who loves you more than you can understand and He wants you to love Him. He made you and gave you life. He wants you to talk to Him and ask Him every day to help you to live as He wants you to live, so that you will be just as happy as you should be."

"He ain't here," he argued. "How can He hear me when He ain't here?"

"God is so great and so wonderful that He can hear you even though He has His home in heaven. He can see everywhere and He watches over you because He loves you."

"Did He watch over my Mommy and Daddy when they put them in that big box way down in the ground?" His grave eyes searched hers for the answer.

The question startled her. He had not mentioned his parents since those first few words as they left the village. His one concern had been about his brother.

"He watches over everyone who trusts Him," she answered, feeling that the answer was not quite adequate, but it was the only thing she could think of at the moment. She feared what was coming, for she felt that it would.

"Is He watchin' over my brother?" he questioned, his lip trembling.

"He surely is," she asserted, confident once more. "And He will keep on watching over him, if you'll ask Him every day to keep watching over him."

She wondered if she had said the right thing. If he remembered to make this request, it would keep his brother constantly in his thoughts and she was hoping that he would forget him in time.

"Can I ask Him right now?" he asked eagerly.

"Sure you can," she told him.

While her heart throbbed with strange new emotions, she watched him as he bowed his head and closed his eyes as she had directed him and then said in earnest tones, "God, I can't see You, but my new Mommy says that you can see me and hear me. Take care of Ted and bring him back to me."

Her eyes were swimming with tears as she helped him to his feet and held him close.

"You precious little darling!" she exclaimed in tones that were quite unsteady. "I know that some day God will answer your prayer."

"But when will He?" he asked from the fold of her arms.

"In His own time, dear. He knows just when that time is best. He always knows what is best for us. Just try to be patient and wait for Him to answer your prayer. I'm sure He'll answer you."

"Is that a promise?" he asked, still doubtful.

"Yes, dear, that's a promise. Some day God will answer you. Just believe and trust Him."

As she put him in bed, she bent over him and kissed him, while a tear fell upon his cheek.

"What you cryin' for?" he asked. "Didn't God hear me?"

"Yes, God heard you," and she gave him a tremulous smile. "I'm crying because I'm so happy. Because I have such a precious little boy whom I love very much. And I hope he will learn to love me."

He held out his arms to her and she bent lower while he put his arms around her neck.

"I love you now," he said, then reached up and gave her a wet kiss upon her cheek.

"Thank you, my darling," she said as she kissed him upon his forehead and turned out the light.

"Thank You, Lord, for giving him to me," she whispered as she shut the door and went to join her husband in the living room. "I pray that he will meet that brother in Your way and in Your time."

Chapter Three

Agnes wondered if she had done the right thing in giving Tag hope that one day he would find his brother. She was hoping that in time the memory of that brother would fade from his mind, for she felt that he could not be as happy as he should until that happened. She knew that it was impossible for her to find the boy.

Each night when she knelt by his bed and heard his childish petition, she was hoping that he would soon forget to voice that prayer. For a time he didn't forget and she prayed silently while he prayed, that the Lord would do what was best for the child.

As time passed and he was old enough to pray without her leading him on, she didn't hear that petition voiced and she rejoiced, for she felt that he had at last forgotten his lost brother and that he could be as happy as she hoped in his new surroundings with his new parents.

Not long after Tag came to live with them, Richard was transferred to New Orleans. Agnes was glad of the change, for her childhood had been spent in the Crescent City and she would be among friends of past years. She was glad also that Tag would be removed from surroundings which might keep memory alive within him.

As soon as they were settled in their new home, she began to take Tag to Sunday school. After talking to the pastor, she decided to have Tag dedicated to the Lord, something which she felt sure had never been done by his parents. If she did this, she felt that she would have a better chance of winning him to the Lord. She and her husband had decided that the child should bear the name

of his foster father and that he would be called Dick rather
than Tag, which sounded more like the name of some ani-
mal than of a handsome little boy.

When she explained to Tag what they intended to do,
at first he objected vigorously. He didn't like the idea of
being led down the aisle and having a strange man lay
hands upon him and pray over him before all those people.
It was too frightening.

Agnes explained that all little children were given to the
Lord if their parents loved the Lord Jesus. She had tried
to explain to him just who the Lord Jesus was and what He
had done for the salvation of souls, but she knew that it
would take time as he grew older to make him understand
fully, something that he had never heard before.

Much to her relief, after repeated explanations, when
the important day came, Tag was willing to obey her wishes.
He felt rather important, to know that something special
was being done for him. He was silent and submissive during
the brief dedication and prayer which followed, but when
they reached home, he said, "Why did that man call me
Richard? That's not my name."

"It's your new name," she explained. "You see, little
boys are often given the names of their father, so we want
you to have the name of your Daddy. Don't you think that
Dicky sounds much nicer than Tag? I like it a lot. It would
make me very happy if you would like it too."

She had found that the child really loved her and that if
something pleased her, he wanted to do that thing. He
considered her words for a moment, then said slowly and
uncertainly, as if he was reluctantly giving up something
very dear to him, "Okay, if you want me to do it."

She gave him a big hug and smiled happily. "Bless
you, my little Dicky. You make me very happy."

She made him understand from the very beginning and
would continue to do so as he grew older, that they were
his new mother and father, for she didn't want him to believe that they were his real parents. Even though he had
been so young when he had lost his real parents and might

eventually forget them, she knew that a tragic heartbreak might come to him, if he should believe that they were his real parents and that some day someone should tell him the truth. Her main concern was that he should become a child of God and that he might be used of the Lord. She would have had this same concern for a child of her own, for it was the greatest thing that she could desire.

As Dick grew older, she thought he had forgotten the prayer he had prayed for so long, that God would let him find his brother. Since he never mentioned his brother anymore, she was sure that he had forgotten, but one evening when she heard him praying aloud as she had taught him to pray, as the door to his room remained open, she was arrested by what she heard. He was asking God's blessing upon his parents as he had done from the beginning, then she heard him say, "And, God, please let me find my brother like Mommy said You would. Please keep Your promise like she said. And please do it soon, Lord, because I'm so tired of waiting."

She was startled and heartsick. How she had hoped that he had forgotten. What would happen to him if God did not see fit to answer that prayer?

Dick was beginning to grow accustomed to his new name and he was rapidly outgrowing his babyhood. He never mentioned his brother, but she knew that he still remembered him and with the knowledge there came a little gnawing worry. She tried to leave it with the Lord, but it persisted.

When a year had passed and there was no word from any near relative of the child, they decided to legally adopt him. It was not difficult to have the transaction completed, after they had presented the facts to the board and the board had examined the case and ascertained that they were fit to be his parents.

The months flew by and merged into years and Dick was now in his teens. The time had seemd so short to Agnes and Richard. She hated to see him approaching young manhood, for she knew that in time he would be leaving them to take up a life of his own with some girl he might want for his wife.

He was tall and slender and was more mature than his age indicated. His little boy beauty had become molded into handsome features, while the golden hair had darkened to brown, though it still refused to lie flat and smooth. Its waves provoked him, but they were the pride of his mother's heart. He seemed unconscious of how handsome he was or of his winning personality. He was quite a boy, for he loved sports and excelled in many of them, but there was a certain quietness about him and he seldom revealed what lay deep within his thoughts.

The one disappointment and heartache that filled his mother's thoughts was the fact that, in spite of her teaching, her prayers, and her attempts to persuade him to yield his heart to the Lord, he would not yield to her plea. There was a seeming hardness and unyieldingness within him whenever she mentioned the things which she believed from her Bible or made some mention of a sermon that the pastor had preached.

He was obedient to her wish that he should go with them to church services, but he sat there unmoved when the pastor gave the invitation after a soul-stirring message.

Agnes spoke to the pastor about it and asked him if he could explain Dick's indifference. He could give her no answer, for he could find none. He advised her just to keep on praying and believing and he assured her that God was not indifferent to her prayers. For some reason neither of them could understand, He was waiting for His own time and not theirs. God alone knew the reason and she must believe and wait upon Him.

"God's time is not always our time," he reminded her. "Remember that passage in Isaiah that reads, 'Blessed are all they that wait upon Him.'"

"I know," she replied, "but sometimes it's so difficult to wait when I see that hardness and indifference growing within him that I can't understand. In every other way he's all that any mother could desire for her son. He's so thoughtful and he shows in so many ways that he loves me. Sometimes he'll come to me and put his arms around me and tell me how much he loves me and how happy I've made his life, but when I tell him how happy it would make me if he would love my Lord like I love Him, he freezes up and won't say a word. It breaks my heart when I see that bleak look come into his eyes. I've said all I dare, for I don't want to drive him from me. I suppose I'll just have to wait and pray and try to be patient."

"That's all we can do," he agreed. "We can't force him to accept the Lord as his Saviour. He has to want salvation before he can receive it."

"I'll try to be patient, but I'll not stop praying," she said as she gave him a tremulous smile.

Chapter Four

The crowd went wild as they stood to their feet in the big stadium and cheered until they were hoarse as the winning touchdown of the game was made by "lightning rod Dick," as he was dubbed by the members of the team. It was the third touchdown he had made in the game and he was literally lifted off his feet and carried to the center of the field by his teammates. They milled about him, congratulating him. They were wild with glee, for this game cinched their chance of being selected to play in the Sugar Bowl at the end of the Christmas holidays.

Dick's face was flushed, not only from the exercise of the rough game which exacted all of a player's strength, but with pride in the knowledge that he had helped to make the winning possible. His unruly hair framed his handsome face in a brown tousled mass. He brushed it back with a familiar gesture and accepted the plaudits of the crowd with a smile of appreciation.

Dick was not only an outstanding student in the senior class, but he was one of the most popular also. His friendly manner and winning personality won friends easily and even those who might have been envious of him bore no grudge against him. In contrast to his love of sports and fun, there was a seriousness beneath his dry humor that was noted by some, especially by his teachers. His mother noticed it more than anyone else. When he was alone and there was nothing particular to occupy his interest at the moment, she noticed this withdrawal within himself that puzzled her. There seemed to be something deep within him which he was not willing to share even with her.

Even in his early college days, he had come to her with all of his problems and had shared with her all of his ambitions and he even asked her advice about the girls he dated. But this other reticence of his perplexed and worried her.

There was still the sorrow which she had felt beneath the joy of having Dick as her own, that he still refused to become interested in spiritual matters. She tried from time to time to talk to him about his soul, as tactfully as possible, but though he didn't put it into words, she could see that her efforts hurt him and sometimes they irritated him.

She remembered the advice of her pastor and she tried to be patient and wait for God's time, but as the years passed she became more concerned and impatient for the answer to her prayers. She knew that as he grew older, temptation would assail him in greater strength and he had no Shield within him to enable him to overcome temptation.

He was popular with the girls and he had many close friends among them. One of these girls was Winnie Hudson. She was not only one of his football fans, but she was desperately in love with him. She had been in love with him ever since she entered college. Dick, however, was not in love with her. He had been interested in several girls, but he had not yet fallen in love with any of them. He was embarrassed by Winnie's pursuit of him. He didn't know how to cope with it.

His chum, Scott Warren, teased him about Winnie, for she made no secret of her interest in Dick.

"That girl's crazy about you, fella. Why don't you give her a break?" he asked.

"Because I don't want to give her any encouragement," Dick replied.

Scott laughed. "She doesn't need any encouragement. She's doing very well without it. If I was in your shoes, I'd give her the works. I'd make her believe that I'd fallen for her as hard as she fell for me."

"But that wouldn't be honest and I'd have to hurt her in the end," Dick argued. "I like her, but I sure don't love her and I know I never shall. She's not my type."

"Not your type! Who is your type, Sir Galahad?" Scott exclaimed mockingly. "You could have a good time with her, even if she isn't your type. Half the fellows in our crowd have had more than one little love affair with some girl until they got tired of her. They know they can't be serious until they're on their own. Why can't you have a little fun like the rest of us? Take that little chicken that I go with. We both know there's nothing serious in our little romance, but we're getting a big kick out of it while it lasts."

"But I wouldn't be getting a kick out of a pretended love that wasn't real. I'd be bored and where would it lead?" Dick asked seriously.

"Who cares? If it lasts, well and good. If it doesn't, one of you would eventually find out that there was nothing to it after all. Gonna grow old waiting for your type to come along?" he asked teasingly.

"Perhaps."

"What if you never find her?" Scott persisted.

"Then I suppose I'll just keep on looking," Dick replied, still serious.

"And end up by being a cranky old bachelor," Scott warned.

"There are worse things that could happen to me," Dick stated.

Scott shrugged. "It's okay with me if that's the way you

want it. But believe me, I'm going to have fun until Miss Right comes along. Then, if things don't work out right for us, I'll have the memory of the good old days and the fun I had to keep me from jumping in the lake and ending it all."

Dick smiled. "Now you're showing you're crazy," and the conversation ended.

It was after the spectators had left the stadium following Dick's triumph and the team was on its way to the locker room that Dick met her. She was standing near the entrance to the locker rooms under the stadium as they were going in. She was with one of the team members who had not been called into the game. As Dick approached with the others, the boy called to him.

"Hey, Dick, wait a minute. I want you to meet one of your newest fans."

Dick turned to meet them and then he saw her. And then he knew. She was not exceptionally beautiful, but pretty, with dark brown eyes, a flawless complexion, a mouth that still held a little girl curve at the upturned corners and a dimple in one cheek as she gave him a tiny smile.

"Nancy, meet Dick James," his friend, John Worth said. "Nancy Crawford is my cousin," he offered as he finished the introduction.

Dick acknowledged the introduction very properly, but his heart was crying out, "Where have you been all my life? And how glad I am that I've found you!"

"I was thrilled at your wonderful playing," Nancy remarked with a smile. "I'm sure that all of the team were just as proud of you as Johnny was."

"I just got the breaks," Dick replied modestly. "But I'm glad that we won. It was a mighty close game and I was afraid that we'd be snowed under. It looked that way in the beginning."

"That's what made it so exciting," she responded.

Her eyes, with their frank enthusiasm for his victory, held no hint of coquetry, such as he had seen in Winnie's eyes and the eyes of so many others, but her look thrilled him as no other girl's look had ever done. He felt like doing a very silly thing and shouting to Scott who was waiting for him nearby, "I've found her! I've found her!"

Instead he remarked that he was happy to have met her, wishing meanwhile that he could tell her just how happy he really was, that at last he had met the girl he had been waiting for. Instead, he added the commonplace remark that he hoped to have the pleasure of seeing her again when he was a little more presentable.

"You'll be seeing a lot of her," Johnny informed him. "She's living with us now and she plans to enter college for the spring semester. She hopes to graduate next year."

"Wonderful!" Dick almost shouted. At least it sounded to his own ears that he was shouting.

"We'll see you tonight at the celebration," he called to Dick as he hurried to join the others.

"Say! What's happened to you?" Scott cried as they went through the corridor together. "You look as if lightning had struck you, but I don't see any clouds."

"It may have been lightning," Dick replied with a laugh.

There were no clouds around, but he was really soaring among clouds that were "out of this world" and there were stars in his eyes, stars that shone deep down into his heart and seemed to be setting it on fire, a fire that he knew would keep burning within him for all the rest of his life. He couldn't believe that things happened like this, but he knew that, impossible as it seemed, it had happened to him.

Chapter Five

When Dick came home after the game, he was whistling a little tune, not under his breath as he often did, but so loud that his mother heard him before he opened the door. She had been at the game and was as thrilled as the others were over Dick's spectacular victory, so she felt that she knew why he was whistling so loudly. She was waiting at the door to greet him.

He caught her in his arms and swung her around the room a couple of times, almost taking her breath away.

"Put me down," she cried laughingly. "You're making me dizzy. I'm just as thrilled as you are over those plays you made and I know that the others are as full of pride over the outcome as you are, but I don't want to be whirled by a madman." Then more seriously, "Son, I'm so proud of you. I felt like going out on the field and hugging you in front of all those people. No wonder you're so happy."

As he released her, he stared at her for a moment in surprise, then ejaculated, "Goodness! I'd forgotten all about the game!"

He caught her hands and his eyes grew luminous.

"It wasn't the game that made me so terribly happy," he told her. "Of course I'm glad we won and I appreciate the ovation the boys gave me, but that's nothing compared to what's happened to me. Give a guess."

He looked into her mystified eyes and there was a smile upon his face that somehow seemed different from any she had ever seen. It made his whole face radiant.

"I could never guess," she said, smiling into his eager eyes. "As your boy friends would say, you're off your rocker, or whatever they say these days about one who has suddenly lost his reason."

"Perhaps both would be appropriate," he said, "It's happened, Mom. It's happened to me at last."

"What on earth is it?" she asked, beginning to wonder just what had happened, for she had never seen him like this before.

"I've fallen in love." He uttered the words with a hushed, muted note in his voice, a sudden new reverence within him. "You're the first to know. I wanted you to be the first."

His words brought joy to her heart. She was glad that he had not outgrown his little boy habit of coming to her with his every little bit of news, either joyful or otherwise.

"Tell me about it, son," she said. "I'm glad for you, if you're so happy."

He led her to the lounge and sat beside her.

"I'm the happiest person in the world." His voice was low and warm and he spoke as if he couldn't believe the wonder of what had happened to him.

"Who is she and how long have you known her?" she asked.

"Her name is Nancy Crawford. I never cared for that name before, but now I think that Nancy is the most beautiful name in the world. I just met her a little while ago. She's Johnny Worth's cousin. She's living with them now. I only said a few words to her, but the moment I saw her and heard her voice, I *knew*. You should see her. She's beautiful, with lovely brown hair and eyes and the sweetest voice I ever heard, next to yours," he added and put his arm around her.

"Don't be carried away on such short notice," his mother advised. "Remember, you've never been in love before, though I'm surprised over that, the way some girls have pursued you. This may be just a sudden crush. You've never had any puppy love, so this may be it. Just be sure before you let yourself go so far that you may be hurt."

"I've already let myself go as far as I'll ever go, Mom. I'm sure, as sure as I'll ever be about anything. I know that she is the one girl in the world for me and if I can't have her, I'll never want anyone else."

She didn't argue with him, but she smiled to herself. She had heard this same story before from others and she had seen them change their minds when someone else had come along and taken the place of the one they had been so sure was the only one. She remembered her own youth, for she had had that same conviction about a certain boy, until he had proved unworthy and then she had met Richard.

"I hope she's the right kind of girl for you, dear, and that if she is worthy, she will return your love. I don't want to see you hurt."

"I know she's the right kind of girl," he insisted. "If you could hear her voice and see her, you'd be sure she's okay."

"I'd like very much to meet her. Perhaps when you know her a little better, you can invite her over to dinner."

He gave her a big hug. "You're great, Mom," he whispered. "I'll do just that as soon as I get the chance to know her better. I'll be seeing her tonight at the rally."

"I'd better be getting into the kitchen to see how dinner is coming along," she said as she rose. "It's late and your father will be coming in soon."

She was glad for Dick's happiness, for she had never seen him so exuberant since he had become the owner of his little dog. The little dog had long been dead, but her memory of that time had never faded from her mind. The little cocker had helped little Tag to adjust himself to his new life and to stop crying for his brother. Now and then she had wondered if he still remembered those first unhappy days or if he had forgotten the past.

She wondered just what kind of a girl she was. How she hoped that Nancy was a Christian, for if she was, she might be able to break through that bleak wall of stubbornness that Dick had raised between himself and her on the subject of yielding his life to the Lord.

When her husband came in and dinner was served, he wanted to know all about the game. He had been able to watch part of it during the last half but was called away from the TV before the game was ended so he had failed to see Dick's last spectacular play.

Dick relayed the information to him while his mother listened with pride in her eyes, but no mention was made of Dick's greater experience.

"I'm proud of you, boy," he said when Dick had finished. "I know the team was proud of you too."

"Oh, I just got the breaks, Dad," Dick said modestly. "The ball just landed in the right places for me."

His mother was a little sad as she saw him getting ready for the celebration, though her heart throbbed with pride as she saw how handsome he was in his tux. She knew that there would be dancing and that though Dick was not a Christian, it was only another of the world's attractions that would help to keep him from the Lord unless the Holy Spirit should bring conviction to him in answer to her prayers. His continued indifference was something she couldn't understand and sometimes her faith wavered when her prayers and tears seemed to find no answer. Often she would pray, "Lord, give me patience to wait for Thy time and Thy way."

As Dick kissed her and went out the door, he was humming a little song in his mellow baritone. Her heart went after him while there was a prayer upon her lips, "Oh, Lord, I pray that if this girl is the right one for him, that she may prove worthy and that she will lead him to Thee."

Chapter Six

Dick's heart was beating madly as he entered the gymnasium where the dance was to be held. Many were there already and his eyes searched eagerly for a glimpse of Nancy. He did not see her at first and decided that he would wait near the entrance so that he might be the first to meet her. A girl as attractive as she would not lack for attention and already a little feeling of jealousy was stirring within him at the thought of her being captured by some other boy.

He tried to calm his nervousness and told himself that he was acting like a little boy suffering from puppy love. But he knew better than that. Although this was his first experience, it was real and lasting. Though it had come so surprisingly instantaneous that he could scarcely believe it, it was there in his heart, as firmly planted as if it had been long in coming to life.

Then he saw her. She was there and, as he had feared,

she was already surrounded by a group of his classmates. His heart sank and that little feeling of jealousy stirred more strongly within him.

He hesitated to join the group. Feeling stupid and awkward, he was afraid that he wouldn't be able to keep his love from showing in his eyes as he looked at her. She was more beautiful than he had first remembered her to be in her simple formal of white, with a little touch of color in the band about the neck which was not too low, just low enough to show the lovely curve of her white throat where it met her shoulders. Her smiling, expressive brown eyes were full of light and laughter as she responded to some quip from one of the boys.

He could hesitate no longer. If he did, those boys would take all of her dances and he was determined not to let that happen. If he did, his whole evening would be spoiled.

As he approached the group, the boys turned and greeted him in a loud chorus, "Hail to the conquering hero!" one of them cried, then the others cheered him until he was embarrassed.

"Stop!" he cried as he held up his hand. "You overwhelm me. I'm no hero, just a player who got a break."

"You know that's not so," Scott retorted. "Just take credit where it's due and don't try to play the modest little fellow, because we know better."

Dick joined in the laugh that followed, but his eyes were upon Nancy. She gave him a smile that made his heart start pounding again.

"I want to congratulate you again," she said softly.

"Thank you," he replied, trying to keep his voice steady and feeling foolish in her presence and angry with himself for that feeling.

"Then you've met Miss Crawford before," one of the boys remarked.

"Yes, I met her on the field after the game," Dick told him.

"You may be in for a jolt, if you ask her for a dance," another remarked. "She doesn't dance."

"Don't you think she should be allowed to speak for herself?" Dick reproved.

"Sorry, chum. Just wanted to warn you not to be disappointed," his friend replied.

Johnny spoke up in Nancy's defense. "I told her that she wouldn't be embarrassed because she doesn't dance. I persuaded her to come, for I wanted her to be here when the awards were given out. I told her that there would be others here who didn't dance, so she wouldn't be made to feel like she's some sort of a curiosity. So don't say anything that you'll be sorry for," he added as a grim note crept into his voice.

"Boy! She's about the best looking curiosity I ever saw, if that is what she feels like," one of the others remarked with a laugh. He turned to Nancy who had been silent during the whole time. "If you did dance, Miss Crawford, you'd be the belle of the ball, as they say, but I wonder if you would let me sit out a dance with you, just to prove that I want to know you better."

"I'll think about it," she told him. "When some other girl turns you down, perhaps I can console you," and she gave him a smile.

The others laughed.

"He'll be in plenty of need of being consoled, if I know Henry," his friend told her.

After a few more quips and laughter, the others drifted away to find a partner, for the dancing was beginning, but Dick remained.

"Aren't you going to dance?" asked Johnny who was showing signs of nervousness, for he saw the girl of his choice across the room looking as if she were waiting for him.

"I'd rather talk to Miss Crawford, if she doesn't mind, so you go on and join Betty who seems to be waiting for you," Dick advised. Then turning to Nancy, "Would you rather sit and watch the dancing or would you like to go outside where it's cooler?"

"I'd like to remain here until you receive the honor that's due you," she said.

"I'm afraid you'll be disappointed in that ceremony," he informed her. "They won't do anything but call me up and make a little speech and perhaps give me a little gold football as a token of my help in winning the game. I'll be glad when it's over."

"You're too modest," she informed him. "I saw how very near your team was to losing that game. You really saved the day and you're entitled to all the honor you receive."

"Thank you," he said. He was glad that she couldn't read his thoughts as his eyes met hers and fixed upon them until she turned hers away. She might think that he had suddenly lost his reason.

"How do you like our city?" he asked as a silence fell between them. "Many people are disappointed when they first come here. They only think of the French Quarter and when they see it in all of its drabness, they are disappointed. The city has to grow upon them before they begin to like it. I wonder if you've had time to visit the Vieux Carre?"

"No, I haven't. I've had so little time to do anything but get adjusted to my new surroundings and to get ready for my transfer to college here. I'm trying to be happy when I'm homesick for the old home and the old life. But I shouldn't say that. I'm thankful that Aunt Laura was so willing to take me in so that I could finish college and not have to start out at once to find a job."

"I believe you've recently lost your parents," he said with a note of sympathy.

He remembered that Johnny had told him this before she had come to live with them. Since he didn't know her, he had forgotten it until now.

"Yes, my mother died a year ago and just a short while ago my father had a heart attack and died very suddenly. I was keeping house for him, but he made it so easy for me that I was able to keep up with my studies. He was such a dear, but he never quite recovered from losing my mother. I never saw two people more in love and devoted through the years, in spite of hardships and privations sometimes. But then they were both such consecrated Christians. I do hope that I can be as they were. When two people love each other and they are both wholly dedicated to the Lord, life is just a little heaven on earth. But I didn't mean to go on talking like this. I'm sorry for boring you. Hadn't you rather be dancing than sitting here listening to me chatter? I won't mind sitting here watching the dancers."

"There's nothing I'd rather do than sit here and listen to you chatter," he said.

The tone of his voice and the expression in his eyes as they met hers gave her a little start of surprise and her heart began to beat a little faster.

"I think you're just trying to be kind," she said, "but I'm sure that there is some girl you'd like to dance with and I won't feel neglected if you leave me and find her."

"There is no special girl," he told her. "Scott and some of the others think there's something wrong with me because I've not had a number of love affairs. Somehow I've never wanted to pretend something that I didn't really feel. I don't want to play with love. Not until the real thing comes my way."

"That is unusual in this day and time," she told him. "But it has also been the way I've always felt. I've liked a number of boys, but I've never really been in love with any of them."

He uttered such a deep sigh that she laughed.

"Did I bring that on? If I did, forgive me."

He laughed with her. "In a way you did bring it on. I was so thankful to find someone like you who has the same idea about love that I have always had — ever since I knew what romantic love was. Scott says that I'm a dope. If so, then there are two of us. How glad I am that you've come into my life, lady," he said with a little laugh in which she joined. "Now I hope that we can be good friends and that we'll be honest and frank with each other. Will you agree to that?" he asked eagerly.

He longed to take her in his arms in front of all these people and tell her that he had found the one he had been waiting for, that his love for her would be as lasting as that of her parents for each other. The longing was like pain within him, a pain that would only be released by the touch of her lips against his.

"I shall be glad to," she told him.

Just then the boy who had asked to sit out a dance with her approached and stood there looking at them with a quizzical little smile.

"If I'm not interrupting something terribly important, I'd like to have the honor of sitting out this dance with you, Miss Crawford," he said.

"You are interrupting something terribly important," Dick told him. "Beat it, boy, and leave us alone. Can't you see that we're deep in serious discussion, not just silly chatter?"

"Sorry, buddy, but you'd better beat it yourself and leave the lady with me," his friend replied with a twinkle in his eye. "How about it, Miss Crawford? You promised to consider my request, unless this fellow has kept you so occupied that you haven't had time to consider it!"

"I have and the answer is yes," she told him. She turned to Dick. "Thank you for letting me bore you. I've enjoyed talking to you."

"I shall return," he quoted in deep tones. "Remember, only one dance, comrade," he warned as he left them.

He was only half way across the floor when Winnie Hudson met him.

"You've treated me scandalously," she chided. "I thought you would at least ask me for one dance, but you've been sitting there all this time with that girl. Can't you have a little heart? I've only this one dance left open. I was hoping you'd ask me for it, so I kept waiting and waiting."

"I was enjoying talking to Johnny's cousin," he told her. "She doesn't dance and I was trying to keep her from feeling neglected. I never thought of asking you."

"My! How very complimentary you are tonight!" she

exclaimed. "You know I'd rather dance with you than with anyone else. Are you going to leave me standing here alone or are you going to dance with me?"

"Come on. Let's dance," he said rather ungraciously, knowing he wasn't being polite, but just then he didn't care. He was angry with Henry for interrupting his conversation with Nancy, and he was disgusted with Winnie for pursuing him so boldly.

When the dance was over, Dick went back to Nancy. There was a scowl on Henry's face as he rose to leave her. Dick wondered what had happened.

"Your friend seems to think that he's the world's great charmer," she remarked icily.

"What made you think that?" he asked.

"He seemed to think that I was just sitting here waiting for him to begin throwing compliments at me and to turn loose his charm upon me. I'm afraid that the girls he has been associating with have fed his ego until he thinks he's irresistible."

Dick laughed. "You've hit the nail on the head. Henry's good looking and has a gift of gab. He has a lot of money to spend on the girls and he uses it freely. I think he has the idea that money and flattery can get him everything he wants and he enjoys seeing the girls fall for him. Money and flattery can do a lot with some people."

"But not the ones who really have the right ideas about life," she stated.

"You're a very wise little person," he remarked. "And that's not flattery, just the simple truth and it makes me very happy. You're the first girl I've met like you and I'm so glad that I have met you."

"Thank you. That's the kind of compliment that I like," she told him with a smile.

The ceremony was short, as Dick had told Nancy it would be. There was a short speech from the coach, praising all of the team for their part in helping to win the game, then Dick was given special mention and presented with the little gold football. Further announcement was made that Dick was named the outstanding player of the season. It was met with thundering applause, then the celebration was over.

Dick sought Nancy when the ceremony was over. Knowing that she was going home with Johnny, he wanted a few words with her before she left. He wished that he could take her home, but he didn't want to rush matters.

"May I see you again very soon?" he asked eagerly.

"Yes, of course," she told him, then she left him, for Johnny was waiting for her.

Feeling that this was the happiest day in his life, he went home. He was hoping that before too long there would be another day that would be even more happy, when, perhaps, at long last he could hold her in his arms and tell her how much he loved her.

Though he had once learned to pray with his mother beside him, there was no thought of prayer that God might make this happiness possible. He had broken the connection between himself and God long ago.

Chapter Seven

Dick was impatient to see Nancy again, but he didn't want to rush matters. A few days after the celebration he phoned her and asked if he might take her out to dinner. His father said that he could have the car. He was quite pleased when she said that she would accept his invitation.

He didn't know that Nancy was almost as pleased as he was, for she had been attracted to him at that first meeting and was as eager as he was to continue the friendship. She had no idea, of course, that he was in love with her, but she was glad that he wanted to continue their friendship. She had never met a boy who wanted just friendship and she looked forward to her friendship with Dick.

Nancy had known what salvation was from her early

childhood and before she was in her teens, she had accepted Christ as her Saviour. Having been taught by her mother, she soon saw for herself from her reading of the Bible that a Christian should not marry one who was not a born again believer, for the one who did that could never have real peace and perfect contentment in married life.

Nancy had been so eager to make good grades that she had little time for social activities. Since these activities among her classmates and friends meant dancing and cocktails, she had no desire to participate in them. Consequently, her social life had been rather restricted, but she was happy and contented in life as it came to her, knowing that she was in the Lord's will and that some day she would meet the one whom the Lord had chosen for her.

The celebration after the game was the first dance she had ever attended. When Johnny had urged her to go with him, she had consented when he told her that there would be others there who would not be dancing and that she would not be embarrassed. She wouldn't feel compelled to dance. She laughed when he told her that and told him that she had never learned to dance. His eyes flew open at that information.

"Whew! You must have lived like a nun!" he exclaimed. "What did you do for fun?"

"I found a lot of things to do — tennis, swimming, basketball, and reading. A person can really have fun in life, even if she doesn't drink or dance, though you may think I'm a 'square,' if that is your latest slang for being a wet blanket."

He put an arm around her and said, "No matter what others might call you, I know you're swell, honey, so just live the way you want to and don't do anything that you wouldn't think was right. I know that you and Auntie were very religious and I'm glad you are, because some of the girls I know surely could do with a little religion."

"How about you?" she asked playfully. "Couldn't you do with a little of your own prescription?"

"Maybe, but let's not talk about it now. Just say you'll go with me to the celebration. Do it to please me. And I know you'll be pleasing a certain party I know. I saw the look he gave you. You just knocked him for a loop. And he's not easily knocked."

She laughed a happy little laugh. She had not missed the look Dick had given her and she was feminine enough to be thrilled by it.

"Then I'll go and sit with the old ladies and enjoy you youngsters wearing your feet out on the dance floor," she conceded.

When she met Dick at the door when he came for her, she gave him the little smile that always started his heart pounding. She looked lovely in her simple little suit of pink. He longed to tell her how beautiful she was, but he knew it would sound like inane flattery and neither of them wanted that.

"We'll get a glimpse of the Vieux Carre," he remarked as they drove down St. Charles Avenue. They passed many beautiful old homes from which they caught glimpses of crystal chandeliers through lace curtains.

"Have you made arrangements for your college entrance?" he asked.

"I find that I'll have to take some examinations. I've begun to study for them," she told him.

"Perhaps we can go sightseeing soon, if you're not too busy," he offered hopefully. "There are some interesting places in the French Quarter after you pass those drab night spots. Would you care to go?"

"I'd like to," she answered. "I've heard so much about the famed Quarter. It should be very interesting."

"We're going to one of the most popular restaurants in the Quarter," he told her. "Arnaud's is famous for its Shrimp Arnaud. I hope you like sea food. If you do, you'll enjoy that. Other restaurants have tried to imitate Arnaud's cocktail sauce, but none of them quite imitate it successfully."

"I do like sea food, so I'll enjoy it," she said.

Dick parked his car in a garage not far away and they walked through the cool autumn evening down the narrow street to Arnaud's. She saw for the first time the fringe of the Vieux Carre, row after row of small houses, some of them looking as if they were ready to fall apart. They were close together, built almost upon the sidewalk, or banquette as sidewalks were once called, with a couple of steps leading from the front doors and with just a narrow alleyway between them. There were heavy blinds in front of the windows.

Women were sitting on the steps, enjoying a chat with their neighbors nearby. Nancy heard their chatter, partly in French and some in French with a "Cajun" accent. Children scampered about laughing and screaming as they played or quarreled.

She watched the scene with interest and just a little aversion.

"Is this a part of the French Quarter?" she asked.

"Just the outer fringe," he replied. "The interesting historical section is lower down, some on Royal and some lower down at Jackson Square. This isn't very attractive, is it?"

"It's pitiful," she replied. She saw an old negro woman sitting alone not far away, humming a tune in a low, quavering voice. Her hair was gray and her face seemed lined by a thousand wrinkles. Nancy wondered what that old woman's life story was.

She was thrilled as they drew nearer and she recognized the melody that the old woman was humming. It was the tune to a hymn that she herself had learned in her childhood, "When The Roll Is Called Up Yonder, I'll Be There."

She couldn't resist approaching her and speaking to her.

"I heard what you were humming," she said. "I know that song. I learned it long ago. It's beautiful isn't it?"

"Yes ma'am, it sho' is," the old woman answered with a smile. "And I believes it. When dat roll is called up yander, I sho' gwine be dere. Praise de good Lord, I's gwine be dere."

"Then we'll meet again some day," Nancy told her in low tones.

Dick couldn't hear what she said, but he saw the smile that lighted the wrinkled face.

"De Lord bless you, ma'am," the old negro exclaimed as Nancy slipped a bill into her hand, then left her and joined Dick standing a few feet away.

He was surprised and quite curious.

"You surely did set that old woman up," he remarked. "She'll never forget you. Nothing like this has ever happened to her before, I'm sure."

"I don't think I'll ever forget her," Nancy said. "She's a precious old soul and she's going Home soon, because she's so very old and feeble. She surely doesn't have much in this life."

"She'll be better off when she dies. She surely doesn't have much to live for here. I doubt if she has enough to eat."

"I know she'll be better off when she does die, because I know where she's going," Nancy said. "She's going to be with the Lord."

"How do you know?" he asked.

"Because she speaks the language."

He was silent. He was beginning to think again about something that had been worrying him by some of her other remarks and by her actions. She was like his mother. That thought worried him. It seemed to make her unapproachable. When, however, they entered the restaurant with its doors opening under the balcony with its columns of iron lacework, he forgot his disturbing thoughts and began to enjoy the evening.

When they had given their order and she tasted the Shrimp Arnaud, she agreed with him that it was delicious. During the meal he was entranced by her conversation. She was quick at repartee and they enjoyed giving and taking little quips that brought laughter to both of them. Others sitting nearby watched them with understanding amusement, seeing their joy at being together, for they perceived a budding romance.

When they parted at her door Dick held her hand longer than he realized. She let it remain in his, for she had no desire to remove it. It felt warm and safe within his clasp.

The eyes that looked into hers glowed with a light under the dim porch light that she could not fail to understand, though she didn't believe that what she saw there was possible. She was sure that she was only imagining something that wasn't there. Perhaps it was something that she wanted to see.

"How about Saturday?" he asked, realizing suddenly that he had just been standing there staring at her while she must have thought him terribly stupid. But he didn't release her hand. "Would you go with me for a little tour of the Vieux Carre?"

"I think that would be fine," she told him as she gently withdrew her hand.

"Thank you. I'll be over about four. That will be plenty of time to do some sightseeing."

He had to fight against the desire to take her in his arms and kiss her. Dick knew that that was what the other boys did, even on their first date, for they insisted that that was what a girl expected, but he knew that she wasn't that kind of a girl. He didn't want to do anything that would offend her and destroy their friendship.

"Good night. It's been such a wonderful evening," he said in low tones, then, after one long lingering look, he left her.

She stood in the doorway looking after him, a little smile hovering upon her lips. In her heart a little song was singing. He was just the kind of boy she had always hoped to meet. She didn't know whether or not he was a Christian and she feared that he was not, but she knew that there would be the hope that if he was not, it could be her sweet task to try to win him.

How glad she was that he didn't spoil the evening by trying to kiss her. But was she glad that he hadn't? she asked herself. After all, wasn't she hoping that he would, even though she knew that he shouldn't? She reproved herself mentally. How illogical could she be? she asked herself severely.

Chapter Eight

Dick thought Saturday would never come. He was like a child, almost counting the hours when the day finally came, until it was time to call for Nancy.

She greeted him with her usual smile and they kept up a constant flow of conversation until they reached the downtown section. After he had parked his car, they started down Royal Street, the old Rue Royal of the French era. They wandered through some of the antique shops and she was interested in the various pieces of furniture displayed in one of them.

He hated to tell her the truth about this place, but he felt that he should be honest with her.

"Many of these pieces that are displayed as antiques were really manufactured upstairs," he told her. "Of course that is not true of many of the other shops, but I've heard that over a hundred pieces of a dinner set have been sold in one shop that were supposed to be a rare piece from the dinner service of Napoleon. As soon as one piece was sold, another took its place."

"How terrible to deceive gullible tourists," she exclaimed. "It's a wonder that your better business bureau doesn't put a stop to it."

"Perhaps they have, or perhaps they can't prove what is being done."

She was intrigued as she caught glimpses of courtyards beyond narrow alleys and behind some of the shops. They stopped in one of the courtyards for coffee, doughnuts and French ice cream. She admitted that New Orleans coffee was rather strong, but she was determined to get used to it. They were seated under a huge umbrella that sheltered them from the warm fall sunlight.

Nearby banana plants waved their long leaves with split

edges in a gentle breeze and she caught glimpses of bunches of green fruit on some of the plants.

"It's a pity they never ripen," he remarked, "but our first frosts come early and kill them. This climate is not really tropical enough for them to ripen. But they render an exotic look that adds to the attractiveness of the place."

"It does. It's beautiful," she commented.

"I've heard so much about Bourbon Street from some who visited here not long ago. Is it far from here? They said it was most interesting."

"Depends upon what interests one," he replied. "We can go there if you want to. It's the next street above here. Then we can continue on down toward the more interesting part of the Quarter."

They turned toward Bourbon Street and walked for a way down it, past several dingy night clubs which were closed, as most of them were during the day. But there were pictures in the window that gave one an idea of the entertainment which would be presented inside when the night life began.

They passed one place which was open, but was so dark inside that one could scarcely see, with dim blue lights burning and far between.

Coming toward them, staggering along, hitting first the side of a building, then almost falling into the street, was a bedraggled, filthy man, thin to emaciation and uttering foul oaths under his breath as he caught himself from falling into the street.

"Is he a product of your French Quarter?" Nancy asked as Dick caught her and pulled her aside out of the way of the staggering derelict.

"I'm forced to admit that he must be," he confessed. "He's a product of the night life on Bourbon Street. Perhaps he's been to the Old Absinthe House. That place was supposed to be the hangout of Jean Lafitte and his pirates when they slipped into the city."

"I remember them and their part in the famous Battle of New Orleans," she said.

"Perhaps some day soon you'll let me drive you down to where that battle was fought," he offered, eager to have any excuse to be with her.

"That sounds interesting. Thank you for offering to take me," she told him. "But I don't think much of your Vieux Carre from what I've already seen."

"We'll walk on down to the more interesting section," he suggested.

They proceeded toward Jackson Square where the statue of Jackson, the hero of the battle, occupied the central place. The square was surrounded by the high iron fence that had been placed there many years before.

"This was the parade ground of the original French settlement," he told her.

He led her into the Cabildo and she was intrigued by the wide stone stairway that led to the upper floor, the steps of which had been worn into hollows by the treading of many feet through the years.

"This is the room where the Louisiana purchase was signed," he told her as they entered the long room where many paintings adorned the walls of the principals of the historic signing that had been made when France sold the territory under the reign of Napoleon. Then they went into the courtyard and he showed her some of the old prison cells.

He asked her if she would like to see the interior of the old St. Louis Cathedral where so many of the prominent French families worshiped and where some of the more famous were buried before the altar. She was eager to see it. They walked silently down the aisle and stood with other tourists before the altar with candles burning and statues on either side. She saw a number of the tourists kneel as they drew near the altar and she observed others seated in the pews, holding their beads as they murmured the rosary while they watched with interest as the tourists strolled silently back and forth.

Nancy was silent for a while as they left the building and started back to where their car was parked. Then she said, "I wonder if those dear people who were so faithful in saying their beads could ever be made to believe that prayer is so much more simple and so much more satisfying and rewarding. It made me want to tell them to lay their beads down and to talk to God just like they would talk to their earthly father or mother."

"I don't think they would have appreciated your effort," he replied. "I know a few Catholics and I know that they are very strict in their religious observances. They are very sure that they are right and the rest of the religious world is wrong."

"I wish that people who belong to Protestant churches were as faithful to what their doctrine teaches as Catholics are to what their church teaches. But if Catholics would only read their Bibles and believe what is written, they would see what salvation means. It isn't doing penance or keeping certain rules. It's a question of the right attitude toward God. It's so simple just to believe and receive salvation."

"You'd make a good preacher," he remarked.

He was quick to change the subject and she was willing, for she knew that he didn't share her interest in it.

She was very quiet and there was a serious light in her lovely eyes during the walk toward the car. He was worried and afraid that he had offended her, but he didn't see how he could have.

"Why so silent?" he asked. "Have I done or said something that offended you? If I have, I'm sorry."

"No, of course not. I was just thinking. Forgive me. I should do my deep thinking when I'm alone and not be a bore when I'm out with a friend."

"I suppose you're thinking about those people there in the Cathedral," he said, then he was sorry that he had said that. It was such a foolish thing to say, for he knew that it was this experience that had caused her preoccupation.

"Yes, I was," she admitted. "I was wondering what their attitude toward God really is. I know that they believe in God and that they believe that Jesus Christ was His Son, born of the Virgin Mary. That is much more than our modernist churches believe. They are beginning to teach their members that Mary was not a virgin, but just a young girl. And they subtly deny that Christ was the sinless Son of God. They deny the blood redemption, deny that one has to accept that fact and depend upon that for salvation. I heard a bishop in a certain denomination declare that he could lift himself up by his bootstraps from the physical to the spiritual. What a far cry from the early church whose members suffered torture and death rather than deny that the way of salvation and eternal life was through Jesus Christ and His blood atonement.

"I was so horrified that I felt contaminated because I had been there and had sat there under that man's preaching. I went with a friend who had told me what a wonderful preacher he was. I'm afraid she doesn't know what good preaching really is."

He was silent and she asked, "Now I'll have to ask what makes you so silent. I hope I haven't wearied you or offended you by my long dissertation, but when I get wound up on this subject, I just don't seem to be able to stop. I shouldn't have sounded off so. Please forgive me if I've offended you. I'm sure I've wearied you."

He uttered a little sigh before he answered her.

"You haven't wearied me and you haven't offended me. You never could do that, no matter what you said. You're perfect, so far as I'm concerned, for so far as I can see, you can do no wrong."

The look that went with the words told her more than mere words could tell and she knew that he intended that they should do that very thing.

She laughed lightly as she replied. "You just don't know me, how very imperfect I am. Perhaps Johnny could tell you that I'm as full of faults and mistakes as anyone else who does try to be more perfect."

She sought to change the subject. "Now that the football season is over, for a while, I suppose you'll be free to take rest from practice."

"No, we'll just have to keep it up until after that game with our old enemy, L.S.U. They're out to beat us and we're determined that they shall not."

When they had reached her home, he said, "How about next Sunday afternoon? May I drive you down to Chalmette, to see the old battle-ground and the famous Pakenham oaks?"

"If you'll go to church with me in the morning," she agreed.

"It's a deal," he said. "Tell you what. You come to church with us and have dinner with us, then we can drive down there afterwards."

"But I can't do that," she objected. "Your mother is the one who would have to invite me and I don't even know her."

"She's already invited you," he informed her with a smile. "She said that I must have you over to dinner whenever you could come. She wants to meet you. She wants to know all of my friends," he added as he saw her hesitate.

"We shall see," she said and then got out as he held the door open for her and walked with her up the steps.

"Thanks for a lovely afternoon," she said.

"It's been wonderful for me," he replied.

As she went into the house, there was a little frown upon her brow. Where was this friendship leading, she asked herself. How far must she let it go? Should she let it continue and what would be the result if she did? She didn't want him to be hurt — and she didn't want to be hurt herself. She decided to pray about it and leave it in the hands of the One who had never failed to lead her along the right path.

Chapter Nine

A few days later Dick's mother phoned Nancy and gave her such a cordial invitation to dinner that Nancy could not refuse.

"I like to know Dick's friends," Agnes explained. "I think a mother should know her child's friends, even if he is no longer a child. And Dick has spoken of you so often that I am anxious to meet you."

When Nancy had hung up, she stood there for a moment thinking. Knowing that Dick was interested in her, she wondered what he had told his mother about her. She could not fail to suspect where his interest was leading and again she wondered what to do about it. Her heart said one thing and her conscience said another. She had no leading from the Lord, yet she knew without that leading that she was treading on dangerous ground, not only as far as Dick was concerned, but for herself.

Her heart said, let this go on, even if it does lead to something more serious than friendship, but her better judgment and her conscience and her loyalty to her Lord told her that it would be the wiser plan not to let the friendship continue. She was afraid that she would weaken if the real test came, but she decided to wait for a while and enjoy a friendship which meant more to her than that of any other boy she had ever met.

It was a bright, sun-drenched Sunday morning when Dick helped her into the car and they drove to his home where they would pick up his parents.

"It's needless for me to tell you how beautiful you look this morning," he remarked as he gave her an admiring glance accompanied by a smile, "for I'm sure your mirror has told you that already."

"No matter what my mirror has told me," she retorted with an answering smile, "it's nice to hear you say it. Thank you."

Dick's mother knew as soon as she met Nancy that she would love this girl. She thought she knew from just a few remarks from Nancy, that she was a Christian. She was happy in this knowledge and hoped that this romance would have a happy ending.

Nancy had never been in their church before, but she knew the moment the service began and she heard the

minister pray, that she would get a blessing from the service.
She took her place beside Dick and they joined in the singing
of the hymns. He gave her a little smile as their hands
touched while they held the hymnal between them. His
heart thrilled as he heard her sing, for her voice was clear
and melodious. His own baritone voice blended with hers
as they sang, but there was a difference in the depth of
their singing. He was merely singing words, but missed the
spirit of the song, while she sang with her whole soul as she
repeated the words of that beautiful hymn, "My Faith
Looks Up to Thee."

The minister read his text from I Kings 8:56, "There hath
not failed one word of all his good promise." As she listened
to the reading of those words, she was sure that she would
hear an inspiring message. She cast a glance at Dick, hoping
that she would see the same response upon his expressive
face. Instead of returning her glance, which she was sure
he observed, he kept his eyes straight ahead. There was a
bleak, grim expression upon his face.

The preacher began with the explanation of what led to
the writing of those words. He gave a brief history of the
time and the reason for the statement. Then he explained
that they were uttered by Solomon after his prayer of dedication when the temple had been completed. He reminded
his people of how God had taken care of them when they
had wandered through the wilderness and that everything
He had promised through Moses had been fulfilled. Not
one word had failed.

As he continued, Nancy tried to keep her attention fixed
upon the message, but she couldn't help wondering about
that look on Dick's face.

The preacher began to apply those words to everyday
living. He explained why every Christian who was in the
will of God had a right to claim and to have faith in the
promises of God. And he gave several inspiring illustrations
from his own life, how God had sustained him in times of
distress when He needed comfort and strength. He mentioned financial needs and how God had supplied his every

need when he had claimed those promises and had stood firm in faith, believing.

He mentioned the promises of the Lord Jesus when He had said that if He went away, He would come again. Then he became more serious and even more forceful when he began to mention these promises and to show how many of the things that had been prophesied had already come to pass, concerning the return of the Lord.

Nancy hung upon every word, for her heart responded to everything the preacher said. She glanced at Dick's mother sitting on her other side and she saw that same rapt expression upon her face that she herself was feeling in her own heart.

On the way home, Agnes discussed the sermon.

"That was one of the most inspiring sermons that I've heard our pastor give in a long time," she said. "He's always good, but today he was better than ever."

"Perhaps he was giving me a special treat," Nancy replied. "I'm sure that the Lord knew that I needed just such a sermon. I'm afraid that my aunt's family don't hear sermons like this. I'm glad I found your church. It's what I was used to at home. My mother would have been thrilled by it," she added while a little cloud shadowed her eyes.

"You must have had the right kind of mother," Agnes remarked with a sympathetic glance.

"I shall thank God for her as long as I live," Nancy replied fervently. "If I ever amount to anything as a Christian, it will be because she led me to the Lord and helped me to live for Him."

Dick was silent during this conversation. Though Nancy noticed it, she had tact enough not to remark about it. But she pondered about it.

The ride home was not long and soon they were in the pleasant living room where they waited while Dick's mother went in to see about dinner.

"You have a wonderful mother," Nancy remarked as

the two of them were left alone. His father had put the car in the garage and had not joined them yet.

"I knew she was a Christian as soon as I met her."

"She's the best," he agreed.

"How did you know that?"

"I just knew. When a person really loves the Lord, it reveals itself somehow. Their very language reveals it."

He didn't reply, for Mr. James came in and a few minutes later they went in to dinner. Agnes and Nancy carried on most of the conversation during the meal which was delicious, while the other two listened. Occasionally Richard would put in a word or two, some jovial remark that made them laugh, but Dick scarcely said a word. Nancy could feel the coldness of his unhappy silence. There was something worrying him. She wondered what it was. Some inner voice told her, even in the course of her conversation, that this friendship should not continue, or there would be hurt for both of them.

When it was time for them to leave for the trip down to Chalmette, she thanked his parents for such a happy time.

Agnes put her arms around her and said, "You have given us a great pleasure, my dear, just to let us know you better," then she kissed her lightly upon her cheek.

"I'll repeat what I've already said," Nancy told Dick when they were on their way. "You have a wonderful mother. You should be proud of her, but I'm sure you are. You must love her very much."

"I couldn't love her more, if she were my very own," he said gravely. "No mother could have been more wonderful to a little lost boy than she has been to me."

"Then she's not your real mother!" Nancy exclaimed in surprise.

"Didn't you know?" he asked. "I thought that Johnny had told you that I was adopted."

"No, he didn't tell me. Would you mind telling me about it, or had you rather not?"

"I don't mind. Most of my friends know it, for my

mother has never made a secret of it. I was just a little
tot when she took me after the death of both my parents.
I can scarcely remember my own mother. I can't remember what she looked like. I used to try sometimes when
I would close my eyes before I went to sleep, and try to
remember the past, but I could only dimly remember a
few incidents and I could never recall her features. I was
so young when she died, scarcely three."

"Did you have any brothers or sisters?" she asked.

Her voice was low and sympathetic and it thrilled him
to know that she felt this for him.

"I had a brother," he told her.

That same bleak look came into his eyes that she had
caught there in the church.

She wanted to ask about that brother, but she was
afraid that she might be prying. Perhaps there had been
something about this brother that he didn't want to talk
about. She hastened to change the subject.

"I'm so glad that you gave me the opportunity to go to
that church," she told him. "I enjoyed the service and
that sermon just thrilled me. I'm afraid that the church
that Johnny's family attends has gone into modernism."

"Just what does that term imply?" he asked. "I've heard
my mother use it, but I never asked her what it really meant."

"I'm surprised that you don't know," she replied.

"Perhaps I wasn't interested," he admitted.

"But you should be. Modernism is apostasy. Modernism
doesn't teach or believe the truth in the Word of God.
Modernists are even denying the virgin birth of the Son
of God and redemption through His shed blood. Now some
are daring to preach this new doctrine that God is dead.
It's horrible."

"Do you really believe everything in the Bible?" he
asked.

"Of course I do!" she exclaimed. "I believe every word
in it just as it is written. What I can't understand, I take
on faith, believing that the Holy Spirit will give me the

understanding that I need as I continue to read it. Don't you believe that the Bible is the Word of God?"

He shrugged. "I believe there is a God."

"Is that all?" she asked in a hushed, grieved voice.

"Can't we talk about something else?" he asked in a pleading voice. "Let's talk about that some other time."

She didn't want to spoil their trip by disturbing him, so she said no more and she tried to be interested in the places he pointed out to her as they passed a few landmarks. He pointed out the Lee monument as they saw it from a distance as they rode along a side street.

"He's one of my heroes," he remarked, giving her a smile. "I've read everything I could get my hands on about him, his life, and the wonderful campaign he waged against the northern armies. I'm proud to say that it was hunger that forced him to surrender and not real defeat in battle. His men were starving."

"That's true," she assented. "He was not only one of history's great generals, but he was a Christian. He gave up so much for a cause that he thought was right. I've always admired what General Grant did at Lee's surrender. His admiration for the courage and greatness of that man led him to permit Lee to keep his sword and he let the soldiers keep their horses so that they could use them to try to restore their farms. In that moment Grant himself was a great man."

"I agree with you," he said.

When they reached the historic site of what was once the Chalmette plantation Dick parked his car and they strolled across the road and under the trees that marked the place of the battle which was fought and won by the citizens of New Orleans after peace had been declared.

It was quiet and cool in the shade under the huge oaks whose branches, weighted by the years, were almost touching the ground. There seemed to be a solemn silence there under the ancient oaks, a silence which the two there could feel.

A few sparrows flitted silently through the leafy branches,

but there was no twittering or angry chirping among them. An occasional mockingbird lighted upon the ground not far away, but soon flew to the branch above without even a quarrelsome chirp. Usually they appeared to be constantly quarreling about something.

Not a sound broke the unusual stillness and quiet as they stood there looking about. It seemed as if they were reviewing in memory the incidents of the battle that had been fought, the natives waiting behind the hastily prepared breastwork of cotton bales, the silent prisoners who had been released from the Cabildo in this emergency, the swarthy sun-burned followers of Lafitte who had offered their services, each waiting tensely for the arrival of the well trained British army.

Then the advancing soldiers rank after rank, looking neither to the right or to the left, but straight toward that crude breastwork.

The sudden burst of fire from those behind that wall that had been deceiving in its seeming ineffectual protection. That cotton held imbedded within its compressed bales, every bullet that was aimed at those behind its protection.

It was over incredibly soon and a victorious group of civilians, soldiers, criminals and pirates looked upon a field where two thousand or more wounded and dead lay behind a retreating army, or what was left of it, while the victorious defenders of their city poured over their ramparts, shouting and relieved of the tension and strain, leaving behind less than twenty dead and wounded to be cared for later. Their shouting was suddenly quieted when they discovered General Pakenham lying amongst the mortally wounded. He died a little later under the shade of one of the ancient oaks.

Dick pointed to one of the oaks and remarked, "That is where General Pakenham was supposed to have died."

"It seems a pity that so many lives were lost when the treaty of peace had already been signed," she said.

"Yes, it does," he agreed.

"I believe this is where the pirates under Lafitte redeemed themselves," she said. "That part of the history reads like fiction."

"I'm afraid that Lafitte was never redeemed," he told her. "One of his men, Dominique Yu, is buried in the old St. Louis Cemetery in the heart of the city, but, according to tradition, after a time Lafitte went back to his old life of piracy and was killed while engaging in it."

"Some people never learn, because they never listen to the truth, but then, unfortunately, many never have a chance to hear the real truth," she stated.

When they returned home it was almost dark, for he had driven her the long way. He wanted to be with her as long as he could. When he stopped the car he sat there for a while, just looking at her until she became embarrassed.

"Thank you for such a pleasant and happy day," she said, breaking the silence.

"It's been wonderful, most wonderful for me," he told her in tones that brought a sudden throbbing to her heart.

When he could delay no longer, he helped her out and went with her to her door. They stood for a moment in the deep shadows of the doorway.

"I've got to tell you something, Nancy," he blurted out. "I know I shouldn't, so soon after meeting you, but I can't keep it any longer. I love you! I love you! I've loved you from the moment I met you. I know it sounds foolish and improbable, but it's the truth. I've never loved any other girl, but I know that I shall love you always. Is there any spark of love in your heart for me? Is there any hope that you could love me? Please say that there is."

She hesitated a moment, then looked into his eyes with a pleading light in hers.

"Please don't ask me that," she begged, "I like you so much, but I'm afraid we can never be anything but friends. Let's keep it that way. Shall we? Please! I wish that I could say yes, but I can't. I can't!"

In her voice was a little cry of pain.

He suddenly took her in his arms and she didn't resist

him. His lips met hers in a long, clinging kiss, then he released her.

"I'm sorry! Sorry!" he exclaimed, then turned away and bowed his head as if he were waiting for a sudden blow.

"I'm sorry! So sorry!" she said in a voice broken by sobs, then she fled from him, shutting the door behind her.

He stumbled down the steps and got into his car and drove slowly away.

When she reached her room she threw herself across the bed while sobs shook her.

"O Lord, I love him! I love him!" she cried, "But I know that I shouldn't! Not as long as he refuses to believe in You or Your Word. Help me! Help me to be strong enough to have victory over this until he comes to You and seeks forgiveness for his soul!"

Chapter Ten

Dick spent a sleepless night, tossing to and fro and when morning came he was not only physically exhausted, but his spirits were at low ebb. He had never been more miserable.

He chided himself bitterly for having done such a foolish thing as that impulsive kiss, but even as he condemned himself for destroying something which he had enjoyed more than anything else in his life, Nancy's friendship, the memory of that kiss thrilled him even in his despondency. The sweet nearness of her in his arms and the touch of her warm lips against his was something that he knew he could never forget.

His mother noticed that there was something wrong when he came in for breakfast, but she said nothing. She was hoping that when they were alone, he would unburden himself to her as he had always done.

His father didn't seem to notice that there was anything wrong and he gave Dick a friendly pat on his back when he passed him to take his seat at the table.

"Well, tell us what kind of a time you had with that sweet little girl," he said after he had asked the blessing. "Did you give her all the details of that battle when you reached the Pakenham oaks?"

"I didn't need to. She knew as much about that battle as I did," he replied, trying to appear cheerful.

"She's a mighty fine girl," his father remarked. "You couldn't find a girl who would please us more if you searched the world over. I fell in love with her myself," he added with a smile.

"I'm glad you like her," Dick said.

When the meal was over and his father had left, his mother remarked, "Son, what's wrong? I know you're unhappy about something. Didn't everything turn out the way you hoped it would?"

"I'd rather not talk about it, Mother," he said morosely. "I'm afraid nothing will ever turn out right between us. I've made her angry and I don't think she'll even want to be friends again," he said in spite of the fact of his assertion that he didn't want to talk about what had happened.

"I'm sure you must be mistaken. It might help if you'd tell me, but don't, if you'd rather not," she added.

"I made a fool of myself," he blurted out. "I held her in my arms and kissed her when I knew she didn't care a thrip for me. She was so angry that she shut the door without even telling me good night."

There was a little smile upon his mother's face. She was wiser in the ways of women than he was.

"I don't believe she was as angry as you think," she declared. "Perhaps she had another reason for acting as she did."

"What other reason could she have?" he asked, surprised at her words.

"Did you tell her why you kissed her?" she asked. "She's not the kind of a girl who would let you kiss her without a very good reason. Did you have one?" She still had that little smile upon her face.

"I told her how much I loved her and asked her to give me hope that she could care for me and she said she just wanted my friendship. She couldn't say she could love me. That was when I kissed her. And now I've spoiled everything. I don't suppose she'll ever want to let me date her again."

She put her arm around him and kissed him on his cheek. He was so like the little fellow he once was, coming to her with all of his troubles and looking to her for comfort which she never failed to give.

"Don't despair, honey. She may not be as angry as you think. Just be patient and give her time. I'm sure she will be willing to be friends again."

He gave her a feeble smile and said in a more cheerful tone, "Thanks, Mom. You never fail me. I just hope you're right."

He was wondering how he could apologize and just how Nancy would receive his apology. He couldn't honestly say he was sorry that he had kissed her, so what could he say and yet tell the truth?

He didn't have the opportunity to see her, for he was busy with practice after school, preparing for the big battle just after the end of the season with their old enemy, Louisiana State University.

When the great day finally came, the stadium was packed with an excited, chattering throng, with flags waving and bands playing. It was a perfect day for the game. The sun shone from a cloudless sky and it was just cool enough to be pleasant.

Dick wondered if Nancy would be there. He knew that during the next semester, they would be attending a couple of classes together. That thought gave him some encouragement that he might be able to speak to her and try to atone for what he had done. He had not felt like phoning her, for he wanted to talk to her face to face, yet he didn't have the courage to ask her for a date after what had happened.

As they sat on the bench waiting for the game to begin, Johnny greeted him.

"Where've you been hiding yourself all this time?" he asked. "Haven't seen you around and when I ask Nancy about you, she freezes up and changes the subject."

Before Dick could answer him, several other players joined them and began to speculate about the game. Dick was glad of the interruption. He didn't know what to tell Johnny.

While the others were speculating about the outcome of the game, he was thinking about Nancy. He was hoping, childishly, that he could make at least one spectacular play so that she would at least want to come and congratulate him after the game.

He was thrilled when the game began and his team was making such good progress, but at the end of the first half they were falling behind and L.S.U. was leading by two points.

During the halfs there was the usual campus entertainment, with bands playing and the majorettes going through their paces amidst the loud cheering from both sides.

There was a tie in the second half of the game and though both sides fought bitterly for a lead, it seemed that when the game ended there would still be a tie. Then Dick at last saw his chance and by his usual brilliant playing, he made a touchdown, and then an extra point for his team. But the opposing team became tougher in the remaining minutes of play. Dick again had the ball. He raced toward the goal, but he was tackled and he went down while three heavy fellows piled on top of him.

At that moment the whistle sounded for the end of the game and the players who had piled on top of Dick scrambled to their feet, but Dick lay there motionless.

The coach and others raced to where he lay and he was taken from the field while the crowd milled about, unwilling to leave until they knew just how badly he was hurt. An ambulance arrived shortly and Dick, still unconscious, was taken to a hospital.

The joy of the home team was killed by the accident, for Dick was once again the hero of the day and they were deeply concerned about him.

There was someone else in that throng who was deeply concerned about him and that was Nancy. She had watched the game with increasing excitement and when Dick made his spectacular play, she was as wildly excited as the others were.

When she reached home she waited nervously and impatiently until Johnny returned and told her how Dick was.

"He's still out," he announced to the waiting group, his mother and father and Nancy. "He's got a lot of broken bones, but they don't know this soon just how many, or if he has internal injuries. I guess that finishes him for any more games," he added gloomily.

"It's just as well if he never plays again," his father commented. "That's a dangerous game. I'm glad you'll soon be out of it."

Johnny turned to Nancy. "I'll take you to see him, if you want me to — as soon as he's able to have visitors."

"Thanks," she said. "I'd like to go."

She was wondering just how she could meet him there before others when that little scene stood so clearly between them. How she wished that she didn't care so much. But, she argued to herself, she had had her warning and she had no one else to blame but herself when she knew that she was falling in love with him. She didn't have to wait to fall in love with him, she admitted to herself. She had fallen in love from the beginning, though she hadn't been willing to admit it. It had come to her almost as suddenly as Dick had said it had come to him. And it was there to stay.

Chapter Eleven

It was several days before Dick was permitted to have visitors. His mother had been with him the whole time. She had followed him to the hospital and waited anxiously for the doctor's report about his condition. He told her that as well as he could predict from the preliminary examinations, he didn't believe that the concussion was too serious. He could not predict whether there were any serious internal injuries until later. The fractures were not too serious.

As she sat there by Dick's bed, she reviewed in memory the years that she had had him as her very own. She remembered what a beautiful child he was and how she loved him from the first. He was so handsome as a young man and she was thankful even in this anxious waiting, that he had not been disfigured.

She remembered how soon he had learned to love her, even when he was so frightened and bewildered, when she had tried to make him feel less alone and forsaken.

She thought of the time when he had first knelt by her side and she had taught him to pray, how grieved she was to realize that he had never been taught anything about God. How grieved he had been because he was separated from his brother. She had been so relieved when he had seemed to forget that brother, that she had never dared mention anything of his past life, for fear that it would bring back remembrance and renewed grief to him.

She was hoping that when he regained consciousness and was on the road to recovery, she could talk to him once more about the Lord and try to make him realize how near he had come to going out into a Christless eternity. It had been so long since she had talked to him about his soul, for she knew that it only made him freeze into silence and that her only hope was in prayer.

She had hoped that Nancy would be the means of bringing him to the Lord, but their friendship seemed to have suddenly ended and with it, that hope.

When at last Dick opened his eyes and looked about him, bewildered, she leaned over and called his name gently.

"Nancy! Nancy!" he called feebly as he saw her bending over him. "Glad I'm forgiven." Then he closed his eyes and seemed to drift into normal slumber.

She sat down again and continued her vigil, waiting until he should wake and be able to talk rationally. She felt a little pang of jealousy that he should call for Nancy instead of recognizing her, but she stifled the little pain as quickly as it came. She knew that some day there would be someone coming into his life who would take first place and she couldn't be more pleased if that someone should be Nancy.

She dozed off for a time, for she was exhausted by the long vigil. She was wakened by Dick's voice.

"Mom!" he called in a stronger voice, "What are you doing here? Where am I? What's happened?"

"You've been hurt," she told him. "You were thrown in the game and injured, so you're here in the hospital."

"What a rough deal that was!" he exclaimed. "How soon will I be able to get out of here?"

"Not until the doctors say you can. The way those fellows piled on top of you, it's a wonder they didn't kill you."

"And just when I was almost over the goal line," he sighed as memory returned.

"So many of the boys have asked about you, but the doctors have said no visitors yet. How I thank God that He saved your life! What would I do without you?"

"You're the greatest, Mom," he whispered as she bent over and kissed him upon his forehead.

"Johnny phoned and said that Nancy wanted to see you

and that they were coming as soon as you could have visitors."

His face became grave. "I didn't think she'd care whether I lived or died."

"Of course she cared. No matter what happened between you two, she would care. She's that kind of a girl."

He gave her a crooked smile. "How do you know so much about her in such a short time?"

"Because she's a Christian and a lovely character. I didn't have to know her long to find that out. And I think that's why you fell for her so suddenly — and so hard," she added with a smile.

"Little good that'll do me," he remarked dismally.

"I'm not so sure that I agree with that statement, but we shall see."

When the doctor came, he was pleased to see Dick's improvement. He told her that they would make a few more examinations, but he felt sure there would be no further complications and he suggested that she should go home and get some rest.

She took his advice and went home, then, before she did anything else, she phoned Johnny, but Nancy answered the call.

"Johnny was so anxious to know how soon he could come to see Dick, that I wanted to tell him that he can come when he wants to now. I thought he'd be glad to know," she told Nancy.

"Oh, he will!" Nancy exclaimed. "I'm so glad to hear the good news. I'm sure he'll come just as soon as he can."

"He would like to see you," Agnes ventured. "The first name he uttered when he came out of that coma was your name. He thought I was you."

She heard a muffled "Oh" and she wondered if she had done the right thing in interfering, but Nancy's reply relieved her anxiety.

"I'll come with Johnny," she said. "Thank you so much for letting us know. We have both been so worried."

When Agnes returned to the hospital, the good news

she received filled her heart with further thanksgiving. Dick had been returned from further examination. As far as could be determined, there were no internal injuries and the fractures seemed to be healing normally.

The next afternoon Johnny and Nancy came. The meeting between the two was rather awkward, but Nancy covered the situation beautifully and put Dick at ease. After Johnny had greeted Dick, she came and stood beside him.

"It's so good to know that you're on the way to recovery," she said with a warm note and a friendly smile. "All of us have been so worried until we knew that you were out of danger. May I take this opportunity to tell you that I screamed myself hoarse when you made that spectacular play that won the game?"

"Oh, then we did win!" Dick cried. "No one ever told me."

"How could they when you were knocked senseless?" Johnny retorted and they all joined his laughter.

"Johnny," Agnes said. "I wonder if you would go with me to the lounge so that I can get some cold drinks for all of us. The doctor said that Dick could have an orange drink."

"I'll get them for you," Johnny offered.

"I'd rather go with you," she replied. "I need a little exercise. I've been sitting too long."

He took the hint and they left the two alone.

"You're a wise lady," he said with a knowing wink as they went down the hall. "Those two love birds need to be alone for a while."

When the door closed behind them, Nancy stood for a moment in embarrassed silence until Dick said, "Won't you sit by me? I've wanted to talk to you, but I didn't know how to manage it before this happened."

She obeyed silently and he reached out his free hand and laid it upon hers.

"I've wanted to tell you how sorry I was because I made you angry. I apologize for what I did."

"Your apology is accepted, so let's let the matter be forgotten," she replied.

"It can't be forgotten," he said. "I said I was sorry I made you angry, but I can't be sorry that I kissed you. I'll never be sorry for that, for I may never have the right to kiss you again, but I'll never forget the touch of your lips, nor the joy of holding you in my arms. I can't forget any more than I could forget that I love you. I meant what I said when I told you I'd never stop loving you. I never shall, even though you never love me. Please say that we can be friends. At least give me that joy. I promise that I'll never overstep the bounds again."

"I'll have to pray about it," she told him. "Perhaps it would be best for us not to have any more dates, but just be friends. Let me think about it and pray about it. I want to do what is best," she added in a tone which she tried to keep steady, but she was sure that she failed, for she longed with all her heart to tell him that she loved him, that she wanted to be more than just a friend. But she dared not, for she knew that she should not.

"Why do you have to pray about it?" he asked.

"Because I pray about every decision I have to make," she explained. "Every Christian should do that. If they don't, they often get into trouble. I don't want to do anything that would hurt either of us, so just let me think and pray about it."

"There's no need to pray, if you think I would bring trouble to you," he said with a tinge of bitterness. "Just forget me. I won't bother you if you're afraid I would cause trouble."

"I didn't mean it that way," she remonstrated.

She couldn't explain the real reason, that she knew if they continued to see each other on dates, it would mean real trouble for herself, because she knew that her love would only grow stronger and that she would be miserable, not only because she knew that she would have to conceal that love, but that she would be doing wrong by letting it grow within her heart.

She was glad when the two returned. It meant that it would not be long before she would be able to leave. The situation was becoming unbearable.

Chapter Twelve

There was nothing that Dick could do but wait for Nancy's decision. He was sure that she didn't love him, or she would have been willing to continue as they had been. This thought added to his gloom and his unhappiness. He had hoped, since she seemed to like him and to enjoy their friendship, that she would respond to his love even though he knew that his ideas of religion and God were different from hers.

He wished that he could do what he knew that she wanted him to do, to accept Christ as his Saviour, but he couldn't, he just couldn't. As he remembered so many of her words about her love for God and how she felt toward God and even her little hopes expressed sometimes that he would believe as she believed and accept what she had accepted, a bleak expression crept into his eyes and his lips set in a grim line. What his mother and what Nancy believed, might be all right for them, but there was no possibility of a change for him.

When time passed and he heard nothing from Nancy, he decided that he would never hear from her. Bitterness and hurt made him so despondent that his mother noticed it and finally remarked about it.

"What's the matter, Dick? You look as if you'd lost your last friend. Can't you tell me about it?"

"Perhaps I have lost the friend I most wanted," he replied after he had hesitated a moment while a deep sigh escaped his lips. "Nancy has decided that we shouldn't be seeing each other any more. She gave some excuse that it might hurt both of us."

"Why should it hurt her?" she asked, but she thought she knew.

"I don't know."

"I believe I do," she told him with a wise little smile. "If it was just friendship that was involved, surely that couldn't hurt her. Can't you see? I think she cares for you."

"Then why does she act as if she didn't even want my friendship?" he asked.

He was so like the little boy he had once been, with that puzzled frown upon his face when she tried to explain something that was far beyond him. She longed to take him in her arms as she had done when he was a little fellow, but she restrained herself. He was a man now and she couldn't treat him like a little child, even though he did sometimes act like one.

"You should know, my dear," she said tenderly and hesitatingly, for her reply involved a subject that was taboo between them. "Nancy is a Christian and for that reason I'm sure she's either in love with you or afraid that she will be and because she believes God's Word, she knows that she shouldn't give her love to someone who is not a Christian. God's Word says that a Christian should not be unequally yoked together with unbelievers. It would be easier for her not to tread on dangerous ground. I think that's her reason."

"Then I'm dangerous. Is that it?"

"If that's the way you want to put it," she agreed.

"H'm. Then I suppose it's all over sure enough."

"But it needn't be, Dick, my son," she argued, determined this one more time to try to make him see what was lacking in his life. "Why can't you yield your stubborn will to the Lord and let Him take over in your life? Just think where you would be now if you had died from that accident. You would have been in eternity and without Christ. You know the truth, because I have been faithful in teaching it to you. Why can't you accept God's love, for He wants to redeem you? He will, if you'll just ask Him. He never fails to keep His promise to redeem you, if you'll just ask Him."

"He never fails to keep His promise?" Dick burst forth. "He never has kept the only one I ever wanted Him to keep. I don't believe His Word and I never shall believe it!"

She was aghast at the bitterness in his voice and the fire in his eyes. It seemed to be the fire of hate that shone from them and it shocked her and filled her with fear. Truly he was on dangerous ground.

"Why, Dick!" she gasped. "How can you say that? What has God done to make you act as if you hate Him?"

"I don't love Him, that's for sure," he retorted. "The only promise I ever asked of Him, He didn't keep. And you said that He would answer me, for He always keeps His promise. Well, He doesn't."

"What promise did you ask Him?" she asked, still more shocked.

"Don't you remember? Even if you don't, I haven't forgotten. When you taught me how to pray, you told me that if I asked God to let me find my brother, He would let me find him. You told me that if I believed, He would keep his promise to answer my prayer and let me find him. I prayed and begged Him every night until I got tired of praying. And He never has answered that prayer."

She sat in stunned silence for a moment. For the time being, she had forgotten that little boy prayer and she had thought that he had long ago forgotten it. Strange, but she had never connected his bitterness and refusal during all these years to accept salvation, because of that prayer. She felt at a loss to say the right thing that might restore his faith, but she felt constrained to try at least.

"I don't know why God didn't answer you, Dick, but I do know that He knew that it was best for you that He shouldn't answer you at that time. Perhaps He was waiting for a time when you would need your brother more, when your reunion might be sweeter than if He had granted your prayer then," she offered.

"I wanted him when I needed him most and I needed him most then," he replied. "Why would He want to keep me waiting for years when He could have answered my prayers when I really needed Ted? What good would it do me now?"

"I can't answer that, but I know that God makes no mistakes and that His way is always best. He answers prayer in His time and in His way and His way is always best."

"That isn't good enough for me," he told her. "I don't want to hurt you, Mom, but that's the way I feel and it'll take time and one of God's miracles that you so often talk about to make me change."

He rose to leave the room, but she detained him a moment.

"I still believe in prayer and in miracles, son, and I shall keep on praying that the Holy Spirit may convince you that you are so wrong and that you are in a dangerous state."

He gave her a feeble smile. "Just keep on praying, if it will make you happy."

As the door closed behind him she dropped to her knees and prayed as she had never prayed before, that the son she loved more than her own life would one day see the error of his ways, before it was too late. She claimed his salvation and told the Lord that she would never give up believing that he would one day be saved.

Neither of them mentioned this conversation again and she tried to act as if they had never had it, for she didn't want anything to come between them. Dick tried to seem more cheerful and he felt that he had succeeded, but both of them knew that they would never forget what had passed between them.

He tried to show her in numerous little ways how much he loved her and once when they were alone waiting for his father to come home, he sat beside her and put his arm around her.

"I've told you before, Mom, dear," he murmured tenderly, "how much I love you and what a wonderful mother you have been to me. My own mother couldn't have been a better mother than you have been."

"Can you remember your mother?" she asked, wondering just how much of his early life he did remember.

She had never asked him before, because she wanted him to forget, for mentioning it might make him remember his brother.

"No, I can't. Sometimes when I realized that I had another mother, I would try, but I couldn't recall her features. You've always seemed like the only mother I ever had, though you've always told me that you were not. Sometimes I wish that you hadn't told me, though I couldn't love you more if I had never known the truth."

"It wouldn't have been fair to you or to your own mother," she told him. "It would have caused bitterness and disillusionment if you had known later on in your life. You couldn't have understood, when you were missing your brother so terribly, if I had tried to let you believe that you were not adopted."

"I suppose you were right," he agreed. "I do want to make you happy," he added.

She reached up and kissed him on his cheek. "You have, Dick, you have. You've never given me one moment's trouble. You've always been obedient and I'm proud of you."

He gave her a hug. Both of them knew that there was one flaw in this almost perfect relationship, but neither of them mentioned it and both tried to forget it, but it lay heavy upon the heart of each of them.

Weeks passed and he heard nothing from Nancy. He decided that she had just wanted to let the matter drop and to let him drop out of her life also. Then one day they met on the steps of the assembly building at college.

He was going to a class and she was coming out. She had been to the Dean's office to make the final arrangements for her entry at the spring semester.

She gave him a smile and he returned it. He was wondering if she would even speak to him.

"I'm finally admitted for next semester," she told him as she hesitated a moment and he stopped also. "I've passed my last examination and I'm so relieved to know that ordeal is over."

"Is that why you never took the trouble to even phone me and give me your decision?" he asked. He hadn't meant to ask the question, but it came out in spite of himself.

"Didn't Johnny tell you that I had been ill?" she asked in surprise.

"I haven't seen Johnny," he replied. "I don't suppose he would have thought to tell me if he had. Probably he thought that we were still keeping in touch with each other. That we were still friends," he added.

"Aren't we?" she asked.

"I don't know," he admitted. "I was waiting for your answer and when I never heard from you, I thought that was the answer."

"I wouldn't treat you that way. That would have been terribly rude. I'm sorry you misjudged me."

"Then may I have your answer this afternoon?" he asked, trying to hide his eagerness. "May I come for you right after my last class and go for a little ride? I promise not to keep you long."

"Yes," she replied with a little smile. "I'll be waiting for you."

"At three," he told her. "Thanks for letting me come."

His heart was suddenly lighter as they parted and he went to his class. It was difficult trying to keep his mind on what he was supposed to hear, and he was glad when that class was over.

Chapter Thirteen

Dick was at Nancy's home on time and waited nervously for her to answer his ring. She greeted him with the same little smile that he loved and they drove out to the lake.

"I promised not to keep you long, so I'll try to keep my promise," he remarked as he helped her in the car and drove away.

They drove along the Bayou St. John and he explained to her that this was once the stream that led to a dock further down toward town. Along the opposite side of the bayou they could see lovely old homes, some of them dating back to the time of the Spanish occupation of the city.

They seemed strangely out of place with their galleries supported by columns and with the pavement underneath, in contrast to the newer homes nearby with their low roofs and modern architecture.

As they drove along the winding road that approached the shores of Lake Pontchartrain, he remarked, "All of this land that we're riding on was once a part of the lake. Over there," and he indicated the ruins of a structure that had long since almost tumbled down entirely, "was once the old Spanish fort. Right where we are now, there was once a bath house built over the lake and over to our right there was a favorite picnic ground. People ate their lunch there and then went for a swim in waters that were not too deep for the children to have fun in. That, however, was before my time."

"How did they accomplish this?" she asked. "This is one of the most beautiful sections of the city that I've seen."

"Also one of the most expensive as far as land and houses are concerned. They pumped the sand from the bottom of the lake, let it settle and fertilized it, then planted these trees. It's a marvelous demonstration of land reclaiming. This sea wall that we're coming to gives protection from moderate winds that bring in the breakers, but during storms, sometimes the water washes over this seawall and some houses are flooded."

Along the wall children were playing on the steps, under the watchful eye of their parents. Even in the cool fall weather, there were groups eating their afternoon lunch under the trees. The gardens in front of the houses beyond the front parkway were beautiful, with roses, chrysanthemums just bursting into bloom, and azalea bushes massed behind, close against the houses. In the spring they would be a gorgeous colorful background for roses which would still be blooming through most of the winter.

Finally Dick came to a parking place bordering the shore, where there were no other cars parked and they could be alone. He stopped the car and turned to Nancy who had said little as he explained the various interesting objects and she admired the beauty of the houses with their gardens and the parkway that stretched between the road and the homes.

"Now we can talk and you can tell me what I'm so anxious to hear," he remarked.

"I'm afraid that I can't tell you anything that I haven't already told you," she began. "I said that I would pray about what you asked me and that I would think about it. I have done both, much, much of both, and I still feel that it would be better if we didn't date as we have been."

"Is that all you have to say?" he asked. "I thought that if you consented to go with me this afternoon, that was a sign that you could give me some good news."

"I came because I promised to tell you what I thought was best for both of us and where we could have a chance to talk without being interrupted. I didn't want to just break off without saying a word."

"Is that the way you really want it?" he asked with a probing glance that caused her to lower her eyes from his gaze.

"No, it isn't," she admitted, "but I think it's best, as I

said, for both of us. I would like for us to be friends as we have been, for I do enjoy your friendship, but the question isn't what I would rather do, it's what I think is best."

"What makes you think it would be best?" he persisted. "I've never been so happy as I am now, since I have known you, but you want to deprive me of something that means so much to me. Is this being kind to me?"

"Yes, I think it is, more kind than if we kept on dating as we have been, for it would have to end sometime and the longer we go together, the more unkind it would be for you."

"What makes you think so?" he asked, stubbornly determined to make her give her reason.

"Because you said you loved me," she said slowly and with apparent effort. "The longer we go together, the more you might think that I'm falling in love with you and in the end you would be more hurt than if we stop dating now. You would have the opportunity to meet someone else whom you could love and then you would forget what might perhaps be only a brief unhappiness, if we ended it now."

"Don't you have any feeling at all in the matter?" he persisted. "Is my friendship or even my love so objectionable to you that you don't want any more of me? Is that the real reason?"

She turned to him eyes that held the mist of tears. "Of course that isn't the reason." Her voice quavered while she tried to control it. "I like you better than any boy I've ever known. I-I don't want to be hurt myself as I might be if we continue to go together."

"You love me!" he declared. "You love me, but you're not willing to give me your love. Is that it?" his tone was demanding, but his eyes were pleading.

"Why do you say that?" she gasped. "I've never given you the right to think that."

"I'm thinking it anyway and I'm saying it," he declared. "If you like me so much and yet you're not willing to date me any more, there must be some other reason than what you said, that you didn't want me to be hurt. You've said that both of us might be hurt if we continued to date. Can you truthfully say that you don't love me? Tell me the truth, Nancy, darling. Can you say that you don't love me?"

She turned her face from him so that he couldn't see the distress that she knew she was revealing.

"I don't have to answer that," she replied in a low, shaking voice.

"Oh, yes you do!" he cried while he turned her face toward him and held it for a moment, tenderly, between his hands, then he took her in his arms and held her while he looked down into her troubled eyes, bright with teardrops.

"Look at me and say that you don't love me, that you don't want to ever see me again. I'll believe you, if that is the truth and I'll never bother you again. Tell me the truth."

She buried her face against his breast and sobbed, "I do love you. I love you with all that there is of me to love, but we mustn't go together again. Our love can never amount to anything. I shouldn't love you, but I do. I-I can't help it," and the sobs became more intense.

He bent down and kissed the top of her head, then he put his finger under her chin and raised her tear-wet face so that their lips met. He kissed her tenderly while her lips answered his kiss, then she released herself and dried her eyes.

"Will you marry me, Nancy?" he begged. "I'll soon be on my own and I swear that I'll do everything in my power to make you happy. I'll spend my life just for you."

"I can't do that. You refuse to do the one thing that would make me the happiest person in the world and since you won't, I can't marry you and I shouldn't even be in love with you. But I can't help that. I fell in love with you before I realized what was happening, but I don't want to go on dating you and being with you, for I want to forget that love, because if I don't, I'll never spend another happy day."

"You mean that because I don't feel the same way about

God that you do and that my mother does, that I couldn't make you happy. Is that it?"

"It's not that exactly," she contradicted. "It's because you will not yield your heart to the Lord. It's not so much the way you feel or think about Him, it's what you do about it and you refuse to yield your will to Him and accept His salvation. Unless you do that, we could never be happy, for I would know that I was disobeying God by loving you and I want to be yielded to His will."

"I was afraid that was it," he conceded in hollow tones of despair. "I can't ever have you because of that one thing."

"But you can, if you'd only be willing to come to God and ask Him to forgive you, just as I had to do, just as everyone has to do, if they receive eternal life. Without that, where will you be and why can't you do that, Dick? It's so easy. It's not giving up anything, it's just receiving the most wonderful gift of all. Without it, there can never be absolute peace in your heart. Why not yield to Him and see if I'm not right?"

"That's a question that I don't feel that I can answer," he said slowly and painfully, "It's something that I don't want to talk about, so I suppose I'll just have to abide by your decision. I can never possess what you call the most wonderful thing in God's universe. Call it stubbornness, if you want to, but I just can't and that's just that. Perhaps someday I may change, but as I see it there's no hope that I shall."

"I'm so sorry," she said with a little sob as she put her handkerchief to her mouth to suppress another sob.

He drew her to him again and whispered, "I'd give my life if I could change, but there would be no use pretending something that I don't feel and I couldn't deceive you by pretending that I will do what you want me to do. Let me kiss you just once more, perhaps for the last time, unless some miracle should happen. And I don't believe in miracles."

She raised her face to him and he kissed her long and clingingly as if he never expected to see her again. As he released her, he uttered a despairing cry, "God! God!"

He started the motor and they drove home with scarcely a word between them.

He helped her out of the car and went with her to the door. As she opened it and turned to go inside, she gave him one despairing look while her eyes filled with tears. Then she closed the door slowly and was gone from his sight.

He stumbled down the steps while tearless sobs shook him. As he drove home, he kept repeating "God! God!" but his cry was not a cry for mercy. It was a cry of bitterness, a cry of a soul in torture, a cry from one who knew the remedy for that torture, but who stubbornly refused to avail himself of the remedy. It was as if someone unseen, a powerful force, was holding him back and keeping him in the chains of the bondage of sin and suffering.

Chapter Fourteen

Dick's mother was anxious to know what had happened between Nancy and himself. She hoped and prayed that the Lord would work everything out between them.

When he came home she had no time to talk to him, for his father was there and she didn't want him to be involved. Though he loved Dick, there was not the same intimacy between them that there was between Dick and herself.

His father greeted him with a smile and nod while he continued reading the paper and Dick went to his room to wait until dinner was ready.

It was the next day before Agnes had a chance to talk to him. She waited until he went to his room and put his books down, then came down for the little snack she usually had waiting for him when he came in early.

He came to her and kissed her as he always did when

he came in. She hoped that something good had happened to him, for he didn't seem as depressed as he had been before.

"I have something for you that you like," she told him. "Had you rather have it now, or would you rather wait until dinner, since it's not too long until then?" she asked.

"I believe I'll wait until dinner," he told her. "I had a late lunch and I've got to get busy with those lessons for tomorrow. I have a heavy schedule. I'll just sit here with you and relax before I get to work."

"You haven't had a chance to tell me what kind of a time you had with Nancy," she remarked. "I'm anxious to know what happened."

"There's not much to tell, but we did get everything straightened out and very definitely."

His voice was solemn and there was a shadow in his eyes that told her that everything was not right between them.

"Don't feel that you have to tell me if you'd rather not," she told him. "You know that all I want is your happiness and if there is anything I can do to help, I want to do it."

He gave her a tender smile. "You're the best mother any fellow could hope to have. You've already done everything you could to make me happy. As I look back on my past life when I was just a little fellow, I can remember so many times when you could have been cross or impatient with me, but you never were. Always compassionate and loving, even when you had to punish me for something that really needed punishment. How I thank you for it. But this time I don't believe you can do anything to help. I've had my ultimatum and I'll have to accept it, but I've determined not to let it get me down. I'm going ahead and live my life and get the most out of it while I'm young enough to enjoy it. And I'll try to forget the hope that I once had of having a beautiful girl for my wife and the mother of my children. Whew! What a long declamation!" he added playfully.

"You mean that's all off between you and Nancy?" she asked sorrowfully.

"Definitely and finally," he stated. "She'll have nothing to do with me as long as I'm the black sinner and the lost soul that she thinks I am, so let's not mention her any more. It will only bring you heartache."

"How about you? How about your heartbreak and heartache?"

"It's gone," he declared. "I've now got a heart of steel, though that's not quite the right way to express it, I suppose. At any rate I've steeled myself, as the poets say, to any further thought of love between that young lady and myself. From now on we're just acquaintances."

"Then she didn't love you, after all," and his mother sighed. "I can't believe that I was mistaken. I was sure that she did love you."

"Oh, she did admit that she loved me. She loves me, but she can't ever belong to me because I'm outside the pale, a lost soul with whom she can't ever have any more dealings."

She was not deceived by the note of forced cheerfulness in his voice.

"You shouldn't talk like that, Dick," she reproved him. "You know that hurts me. I'm so sorry, so very sorry that you can't measure up to her attitude toward God."

"There's no use of being sorry, Mom," he replied seriously. "What's happened, has happened. I am what I am and I don't see how I can change, so let's forget it all and try to be happy in forgetting."

"I can't understand you, Dick," and she regarded him gravely. "I did everything in my power to lead you to the Lord. I wonder where I've failed. I would give my life if I could change you."

"You never failed me, Mom," he said gravely. "Don't make me say it. It wasn't you."

"You mean that it was God," she said and there were tears in her eyes. "Oh, my child! Can't you see that whatever God does is best? He hasn't failed you. If He didn't keep that promise in the way you thought He should have done, what He did was for the best. He may still have something so much better for you in the future, if you'll only trust Him."

"Let's not talk about it anymore. I just can't," he told her. "I don't want to hurt you, but the way I feel is something that I don't seem to want to change, so let's let it rest there."

"I can't let it rest there," she contradicted, "and I shall never stop praying that one day you may see how wrong you are."

"Keep right on, if it will make you happy," he advised.

"Dick," she persisted, "you're like so many others, people who have said they believed God, yet when the first trouble or heartache came, they moaned, 'Why has God treated me like this?' and they grow bitter and turn away from God. You're just like them, but, remember, son, some day you will be called upon to give an account of yourself to the God who made you and what will your answer be?"

"Don't ask me, Mother," he said sadly. "I don't know."

He rose and remarked that he must get to his books. She watched his athletic figure as he walked from the room and a sob broke through her lips.

"Lord, what can I do, what can I say? Oh, take over, Lord, and bring Him to Thee in Thy way and Thy time," she murmured.

As the days passed and Dick seemed so cheerful and seemed to be enjoying life as he never had before, she wondered about it. There was a hard shell of gaiety about him that she knew must be a false front to hide a hurt that was eating at his heart, but he gave her no opportunity to say more than she had said and she knew that there would be no use for her to say more than she had said. She would have to leave it with the Lord and place Dick in His hands. She tried to be patient, but she found it very difficult. She kept repeating a part of a verse in Isaiah that she loved, "Blessed are they that wait upon Him." She felt that it was speaking for her.

Dick was seldom at home on week ends. This was

something new, but Agnes asked no questions. She knew that she couldn't treat a twenty-year-old boy as she had done when he was a little child. Even though he wasn't a Christian, she had faith enough in him to know that she need not fear that he would get into trouble.

In spite of her attempt to leave her problem in the Lord's hands, she continued to worry about it and to grieve over it. She finally decided that she would have a talk with Nancy. Though she had thought of it and rejected the idea before, now she decided to act. She phoned Nancy and asked her to come over and have lunch with her. Since Dick was away, there would be no danger of his coming in and finding Nancy there.

At first Nancy hesitated, wondering why this invitation was given, but when Agnes explained to her that she just wanted to have a little talk with her and told her frankly that it was about Dick, that perhaps Nancy could help her, she finally said she would come.

Nancy felt a little embarrassed when she was greeted by Agnes, but when Agnes began to tell her why she had asked her to come, her embarrassment disappeared.

"I felt that I had to talk to you," Agnes began. "I'm so worried about Dick. I know how much he loves you, my dear, and I had hoped that you might be able to help me about what has happened between you two."

"I don't see that there is anything that I can do to help, but I'm only too willing to try," Nancy told her. "I learned to love you even though we've seen each other so little."

"I can see why Dick fell in love with you," Agnes told her. "He's never been in love before, but I suppose he's told you that already. Though he pretends not to be hurt by what has happened, I know that his heart is broken."

"Then you know what happened," Nancy remarked.

"Yes," Agnes admitted. "I sort of pulled it out of him. He's like a little child about some things, even yet. He still comes to me with his troubles and his problems and I knew after his last date with you that something was wrong and he finally told me."

"Then you know I couldn't have done anything other than what I did."

"I know you were right in not letting your love lead you into breaking God's will for your life and I admire you for it," Agnes told her. "I thought that perhaps you might be able to do for him what I've never been able to do. I think that perhaps if you know his story, you might understand him better and you might be able to pray with more understanding than if you didn't know all the facts."

"I know that Dick was adopted. He told me that," Nancy told her.

"But did you know that he was a twin?"

"No," Nancy replied, surprised. "He said he had a brother, but he didn't seem to want to talk about him and I didn't pry. I thought there might have been something wrong about their relationship."

"I took Dick when he was barely three. When the two children were separated, it was very hard for me to make him forget his brother. In fact he never did, but as time passed I thought he had. When I first took him, he ran away to try to find his brother. We tried to locate the child, but the family who had taken him moved away and no one knew where they were.

"I made what was perhaps an unfortunate promise that if he would ask the Lord to let him find his brother, that the Lord would let him find him. I said that the Lord always keeps His promise to answer the prayer of faith. I don't know when he stopped praying, for when he grew older I didn't listen to him pray aloud. I sometimes wonder if he prayed at all. When he didn't find his brother, through the years he grew bitter, for he holds that against the Lord. He told me so not long ago. That has been the reason that he never would yield to my persuasion for him to accept the Lord. God hasn't kept His promise, so he'll have nothing to do with God."

"That's terrible," Nancy remarked. "It's unusual for a child to grow bitter toward God. When they are young it's so easy to lead them into faith and salvation."

"I don't know how old he was when he became so bitter. He always went to church with us and it wasn't until he was older that he seemed so adamant when I tried to lead him to the Lord. I thought that if you understood just why he is like he is, you might join me in prayer and that you could pray with more understanding."

"Thank you for telling me," Nancy told her. "I've been praying for him ever since I first met him, for I didn't believe that he was a Christian. I love him very much." Her eyes filled with tears. "It tore my heart to give him up, but there was nothing else that I could do. I still believe that I can never love anyone else as I love him. And I still believe that God is able and willing to keep His promise."

"Sometimes it's hard to be patient and wait," Agnes said as she uttered a sigh.

"I'm so glad that you asked me to have this talk with you, for I often wondered why Dick was so hard and unyielding. It helps to know the reason, even though it does seem so improbable."

When she had left, both of them felt better and they had the courage to keep on praying and believing for Dick.

Chapter Fifteen

One afternoon when Dick came out of one of his classes, he came face to face with Winnie Hudson. He hadn't seen her for weeks and had almost forgotten her while he was involved with Nancy.

He smiled at her, but she greeted him with a slight nod and meant to pass him by without speaking.

He stopped her and asked, "Why the icy greeting? Am I in the doghouse?"

"Don't you think you should be?" she asked in cold tones.

"After the way you've treated me, you should be in the doghouse."

"Isn't there any forgiveness in your heart, lady?" he asked playfully, pleading. "What can I do to apologize and to tell you that I'm really sorry if I have offended you? I've only been trying to be nice to a girl who was a stranger and a cousin of one of my closest friends. I was just trying to make her feel at home."

"It's taken you quite a time to make her feel at home," she retorted.

"Perhaps I'm a slow worker," he quipped. "What can I do to recover your good will?"

"I don't know that you can do anything," she stated. "A girl ought to know when she's been given the gate, if you'll pardon the expression."

"But you haven't," he argued. "Would you be willing to go with me tonight to a movie, or else just for a ride? I'd be obliged to you, kind lady, if you would give me the honor of your presence."

"What's happened?" she asked unsmilingly. "Has your girl friend given you the gate?"

"Would you believe me, if I told you that we were only friends and that we're still just friends? I'm still waiting for your answer. May I call for you tonight? Do say yes."

"I suppose I shouldn't, but I'll say yes," she conceded. "I shouldn't pass up the opportunity of going out with the hero of the season."

"That isn't very complimentary to my lovable personality," he said with a grin, "but I'll say that I'm pleased that you're willing to go with me, no matter why."

She smiled at last. "You're still the same old Dick. You can't change. Thank you for inviting me."

He watched her go and a smile played about the corners of his lips. She still cared, for she couldn't hide it. Perhaps life wouldn't be so dull after all.

They went for a ride together, for that was what she preferred and they talked of everything but the one thing that was on Winnie's mind. That was what had happened between Nancy and himself. She longed to ask, but she dared not. He was so gay and entertaining that she didn't want to bring an end to his mood. Though he had never asked her for a date before, she had hinted at it many times. Whatever trouble there was between Nancy and himself, she didn't mind. In fact she was glad. Even if he did turn to her on the rebound, she was glad to accept his attentions, for she still loved him though he had made her angry when he had ignored her for so long.

When he returned her to her home and before they parted at her door, he took her in his arms and kissed her. She was surprised and thrilled, even though she knew that he had done it because he thought she expected it. Others had done the same thing, but not on their first date. She had let them, not because she cared for them, but because she wanted to be popular with others, even though she was in love with Dick. Putting her arms around his neck, she kissed him again, then flew inside after a murmured good night.

Dick stood staring at the closed door. He thought that he shouldn't have kissed her. He felt ashamed of himself for having done something that he had never done before with all the other girls he had had dates with, violating a principle which he had always had. But after a moment he shrugged, then turned and ran down the steps and drove home.

He and Winnie were together often after this and Winnie's hopes were beginning to be revived. She hoped he was falling in love with her. Perhaps at last her love was winning him, in spite of her despair. She was supremely happy and Dick did nothing to dispel her hopes.

Others began to notice and finally Scott remarked about it.

"I see you're taking my advice and playing the field. Giving Nancy the grand rush and then giving Winnie the same treatment."

"Might as well, don't you think? You gave me good

advice. It works. I've found that in numbers there is safety," Dick retorted.

"What'll Nancy think, now that you're giving Winnie the grand rush?" Scott quizzed.

"What does it matter? We're just friends. What chance would I have to try to make it anything more than friendship when I still have six months of school and then have to look for a job?"

"Wise decision, my boy," Scott told him. "But I just can't accept that explanation. If there's been trouble, I'm sorry, but then you know the old saying that the course of true love never runs smooth."

"Let's leave it there, shall we?" Dick advised.

"Just don't break Winnie's heart," Scott said seriously. "She's a fine girl and she deserves better treatment from you. I think a lot of her, but she never would give me a second glance. She had eyes only for you."

"I'll tell her how you feel," Dick said with a wicked little smile. "I'm sure that will make her happy."

"You do and I'll brain you," Scott warned as they parted and waved to each other.

As Dick continued to show Winnie attention, he realized that he had gotten himself into a tight spot. She seemed to take it for granted that he was in love with her. Kissing her had become a habit, for he saw that she expected it. He despised himself for leading her on, but he excused himself by saying that it was what other boys were doing.

He wondered when Scott had become interested in her, but he didn't care what Scott felt or what Winnie might feel when she finally knew the truth, that he didn't care for her. Unconsciously he was giving vent to the bitterness and the hopelessness within him over his own heartbreak. What she might suffer didn't matter.

She had hinted of her love for him so often that he wondered how he could keep from telling her the truth, but she seemed to take it for granted that he loved her and he thought he'd just let her go on as long as she was happy in the idea.

When Christmas came he knew that she would expect him to give her a gift. He asked his mother what she would suggest, but what she suggested didn't appeal to him. He finally decided on a little locket upon a beautifully carved chain. It was more than he felt he could afford, but he spent the money anyway.

When she saw the little box that contained the locket, she uttered a pleased little gasp and her eyes were shining. She threw her arms around him and said, "Oh, Dick, you know how much I love you. You don't know what this means to me, to get this — this"

"Hadn't you better open it," he interrupted, aghast as he realized that she thought it contained a ring.

When she saw what was in the box, she couldn't conceal her disappointment.

"Thank you," she said, trying to keep her voice steady. "It's beautiful," then she burst into tears.

"What have I done?" he asked, though he knew that she had been disappointed because it wasn't a ring.

"Nothing," she said, wiping away the tears.

He took her in his arms and she buried her face upon his breast.

"I — I thought you cared enough to — to —"

"I understand," he said, feeling trapped and not knowing what to say. "You thought I was giving you a ring. Is that it?"

She nodded. "I thought you cared enough. You've known how much I care."

"But Winnie, I can't be engaged to anyone now. Don't you understand? I've got to finish school. Then I'll have to look for a job. Can't we be just friends until I can have something to offer a girl?"

"We could at least be engaged, even if we couldn't be married for a long time," she suggested. "You never have come out and said you loved me. Perhaps you don't. Do you?"

"I want us to be friends for now," he evaded. "I don't believe in long engagements and I'm never going to tie a girl down by telling her that I love her until I'm able to marry her and give her the kind of support she's entitled to," he said firmly. "Now, honey, if you don't want that little gift, I'll take it back and we can still be friends. But I was hoping that you would like it."

"I do," she said, raising her head and releasing herself from his arms. "I shall wear it and just hope that nothing will ever come between us."

When he left her he felt more like a heel than ever, but he shrugged again and tossed off the accusing thought. If she was so dumb, then let her bear the consequences. When she found out the truth, perhaps she would turn her attention to someone else. He was not willing to think of what she might suffer when she knew the truth. Rather, he was concerned about his own suffering and the effort he was making to forget it. That he would perhaps be breaking a young girl's heart in the process didn't concern him in the least.

Nevertheless, when he returned home to the quiet time he would have with his parents and a few friends who had been invited to dinner, there was a grave light in his eyes and a guilty feeling in his heart.

Chapter Sixteen

As graduation time drew near, Dick pursued his reckless abandonment to the pursuit of any momentary pleasure that would fill in the hours and keep him from thinking. He tried to tell himself that he was having the time of his life, that he had missed much in the past and now he had at last come to a sane way of living. But in his quiet moments when he was trying vainly to sleep, he knew that he wasn't fooling himself at all. He was only trying unsuccessfully to cure an ache that persisted in his heart and he wondered if time would ever bring release.

He had tried playing the field as Scott had suggested, dating different girls, but instead of having a happy time, he was more often bored. Nancy had always been entertaining as well as lovable. There was always something interesting in what she said, even if it sometimes made him uneasy when she talked about God and her faith in Him. These other girls had nothing but silly chatter to offer and he was glad when he could take them home and forget to ask for another date.

At first Winnie was hurt and angry and she pouted whenever she was with him. She had assumed the attitude that he belonged to her exclusively. He made her understand very politely, but very firmly, that since they were not engaged, he was not bound to her by any tie and that he should have the right to date others. And he advised her to do the same.

"But I don't want to go with anyone else," she informed him. "I want only to be with you. You should know that by now."

He admitted to himself that he surely should know. She had made that very evident for a long time.

"Why don't you take a second look at Scott?" he suggested. "He cares for you, but he said you wouldn't even give him a glance."

"Why should I when I have you?" she asked, smiling archly.

"But you could make him happy for a little while," he argued.

For a moment, she was thoughtfully silent, then she said, "I might consider it. He is really good looking."

She was thinking that perhaps this little game he was playing might work both ways. Perhaps he might be jealous if he saw her with someone else who cared.

He had seen little of Nancy during this time, for though they were in some classes together, they seldom met. Wondering if Nancy had planned it this way, and he was sure that she had, made him angry with her, and added to his unhappiness.

One day when he and Winnie were coming from one of their classes, they met Nancy face to face. Winnie had to hurry, for she was late for her next class and she had to leave them together, though she hated to do so, for she was still very jealous of Nancy. She had tried several times to find out what the trouble was between them and she finally asked Dick to tell her what it was. He told her that he didn't want to talk about it and that silenced her.

Nancy gave him a smile and said, "Hello."

He would have passed her without an answering greeting, but she stopped him.

"Is there any reason why you should refuse even to speak to me?" she asked.

"Don't you think there is?" he retorted. "You gave the orders and I'm only trying to obey."

"But do we need to be enemies?" she asked sadly. "Can't we at least be friends with a speaking acquaintance?" She gave him a smile that was wistful and pleading, one that brought the desire to take her in his arms and a keener stab of pain assailed him as he observed that wistful expression in her eyes.

"I'm afraid, my lady," he said with the shadow of a smile, "that just a speaking acquaintance isn't satisfactory. With me, it's all or nothing."

Her eyes clouded. "I'm sorry if that's the way you feel," she murmured, then passed him and went on her way down the hall.

In the class that followed he had difficulty keeping his attention fixed upon a very important lecture even though he had to take notes in preparation for one of the final examinations.

That night he tossed restlessly and tried vainly to sleep, but it was almost morning before he fell into a troubled slumber. He reviewed the past few months since that last talk with Nancy when she had made him understand that there could be nothing between them as long as he refused to accept salvation.

He had been following a will o' the wisp, seeking something that could not be found, that all of his reckless search after happiness with a different girl in his arms and her lips upon his, had been foolish and had brought him nothing but contempt for himself. Dick had been trying to forget something that could not be forgotten. But it didn't make him any more willing to accept the only way out of this slough of misery and pain.

He wondered at his own stubbornness and why he was so hard and unyielding to the one thing that would bring back the joy he had hoped for in Nancy's love. The story of Pharaoh that his mother had told him when he was a little fellow came back to his mind, and how she had tried to explain why all the punishments had been poured forth upon Pharaoh and his kingdom. She tried to make him understand that God did not harden Pharaoh's heart until this king had defied God and had cried, "Who is the Lord God that I should obey His voice?" He had hardened his own heart and refused to obey the command that God had given Moses, then God had allowed his heart to become more hardened and he was doomed to destruction.

Dick tried to remember just when he had begun to cease praying that God would keep His promise, when this bitterness of disappointment had first begun to possess him. Then he did remember. It had been in Sunday school. His teacher had been telling the children the story of Joseph and how he had been put in prison and afterward delivered. How God had taken care of him.

Dick had burst out in his childish enthusiasm, that God was going to take care of him and let him find his brother, because his mother had told him that if he asked God and believed, God would keep His promise to answer his prayer. He always answered prayer.

The teacher had smiled at his enthusiasm. She told him that he must not take that promise so literally. She had tried to explain what she meant.

"You see, Dick, this story about Joseph was way back there when people didn't know as much as they do today about the Bible. We can't believe like those people believed way back there, for we're more enlightened. We know better. These stories are wonderful, but we can't act on them now. You shouldn't expect God to perform miracles for you today like He did way back there in the past. God doesn't do things like that today. We just have to do the best we can and then do what a little saying reads, 'Hope for the best, get ready for the worst and take what God sends.' "

"You mean that God won't keep His promise to let me find my brother?" he asked as his hope and his faith began to waver. "But my mother told me that God would, even if it was a miracle."

The teacher smiled. "Your mother just wanted to keep you happy, I'm afraid. Perhaps she still has the old fashioned way of taking the Bible just like it's written. You see, today we know that it is full of wonderful stories and symbols and that it is good for us to read it, but we can't believe everything just as it's written. We have to interpret it according to the way we see it. You just be a good little boy and leave everything to work out for the best and don't look for miracles or you'll be disappointed."

She gave him a little pat on his head and some of the children giggled while Dick remained silent, pondering her words and for the first time doubting his mother's wisdom and her honesty. He had gone home with the firm conviction that his mother was not correct when she had believed that God would even perform a miracle if he would keep on praying and believing.

He remembered that from that day on he had stopped praying and believing and it was under the false teaching of this Sunday School teacher that a little seed of bitterness had been planted within him when he had lost faith in prayer.

Dick didn't blame his mother. He just thought that she was mistaken, as the teacher had told him. But he had kept this hidden within his heart. He didn't want to confess to his mother that she had been wrong, because she didn't know any better. Young as he had been, he loved her too much to make that confession. But the seed of bitterness grew.

That teacher would never know until all things were revealed when it was too late for her to correct the evil she had planted in the heart of a little child, the evil of disbelief. It would also never be known how many other such teachers along the way had destroyed faith in others under their ministry of modernism.

As Dick grew older that doubt and bitterness had grown with the years and though he saw the result of real Christian faith in his mother and others, only the unseen power of the Holy Spirit could uproot that bitterness and lead him to faith.

When Dick realized how foolish and unsuccessful he had been in the way he had pursued to try to help him to forget, he became more moody and unhappy. He abandoned his reckless pursuit after pleasure and spent his spare time in reading and study.

Graduation came and he had his desire fulfilled, for he graduated with honors. At last he was free and on his own and he could look for a position that would be in line with what he had chosen for his career — electronics.

Winnie had at last come to the conclusion that Dick had no intention of becoming engaged to her and she finally took his advice and began to look to Scott for some attention. Scott responded happily and they were together frequently, for which Dick was thankful. This would relieve him of the necessity of telling her the truth, that he didn't love her. He hated himself for having led her on, though he tried to excuse himself. Through the friendship of his teacher and the good recommendation he gave Dick to the head of a firm in town, he obtained the position he had hoped for. He was sent to headquarters before he started to work, for further study and to become accustomed to the work and its routine before taking up his position in the New Orleans plant.

Dick was glad of the opportunity to get away for a while. It would take him away from everything that was associated with Nancy and he hoped that when he returned, he would have overcome his love and the unhappiness that he had endured.

Chapter Seventeen

Dick was relieved to know that when he left, he wouldn't have to have a farewell scene with Winnie. He was glad for Winnie's sake as well as his own that she and Scott seemed to be interested in each other. Though he had tried to ignore it, he was glad to be out of a situation that had caused him such a twinge of conscience. Though he had gotten so far away from God, he had not forgotten his mother's teachings and one of them had been to be honest and sincere with the girls he dated.

He was hoping that he might meet Nancy and that he could tell her that he was going away, but he did not see her. But, he thought, why should it make any difference to her whether he went away or not? She had put him out of her life, so he should try even harder to put her and thoughts of her out of his life. It was easier to ask the question and to determine that he would obey his desire to do that very thing, than it was to accomplish what he longed to be able to do.

His mother had a talk with him before he left.

"I shall miss you so much," she told him while tears came to her eyes and her voice betrayed what she was trying to conceal from him. "This will be the first time we've been separated and I shall be lonely without you. You've been such a precious part of my life for so long that it'll be hard to go on without you. I'll feel that a part of me has gone."

He put his arms around her and said playfully, "Oh

Mom, is that all I am, just a part of your life, like eating breakfast and washing dishes? I thought I was really somebody. How small you make me feel."

"You know what I mean," she corrected him with a little laugh. "I'll repeat what I've said so often. You've been the best son that any mother could ever want and you know that I love you as much as if you were my own flesh and blood. I'm so thankful to the Lord for letting me have you."

"You know what I think of you, because I've told you often enough," he said tenderly. "I couldn't love you more if I tried. I'm so glad that you wanted me and took me and you've made my life happy all these years. But don't feel as if I'm never coming back. I'll only be gone a few months. When I come home, I'll be able to begin to pay you and Dad back for all you've spent on my education."

"We don't want to be repaid, Dick," she told him. "We're just glad that we were able to do that for you."

"But still it'll come in handy when you and Dad are old and he is retired. You can sit by the fire and take it easy and not have to worry about a single thing."

"I'm only worried by a single thing now, Dick, and that is you," she told him, meeting his laughing eyes with her serious ones. "I'm afraid of what might happen to you in that big city where there are so many temptations. If I was sure that you were a Christian, I'd feel safe about you, but now I just don't know."

"If you're afraid I'll go to the dogs, don't be," he said seriously. "I can at least do what you have taught me about morals, I shall keep my self respect, so don't worry about that, please."

"That's not what I mean and you know it. I'm thinking of your soul, Dick. What if something might happen to you? You're not ready to meet God."

He put his finger over her lips. "Now, none of that. I thought we decided not to mention that any more. There's my taxi. Good-by, Mom, dear, and take care of yourself. And kiss Dad for me."

He gave her a swift kiss and took up his bags and hurried out of the door to the waiting taxi.

As she watched him go, tears fell from her eyes. She had forgotten to ask him to promise to go to church. Would he go since he would not have to go with her to please her?

Turning away from the window, she uttered a prayer that God would keep him safe and that in some way which He alone would be able to accomplish, that hard heart of Dick's might be broken, if necessary, in order that his soul might be saved.

Dick found his new work both interesting and absorbing. He became familiar with what he was to accomplish in a short time, to the satisfaction of those who were in charge of his schooling with the company.

There were several girls working in the business office and he was on friendly terms with them. Two of them were quite attractive and he was able to have dates with each of them. They knew that there was nothing but friendship in his attentions and they were satisfied to keep it on that basis. Dick was both handsome and entertaining and they enjoyed his companionship.

When Sunday came after he had dated one of the girls a few times, she asked him if he would go to church with her and have dinner with her and her family afterward. He accepted her invitation eagerly. He had not gone to church since he had left home and Sunday proved to be a rather dull day after he had seen the interesting sights of the city and had attended a few shows which bored him. Dick was glad to have the opportunity of being with a family again, even though they were strangers.

Helen Daniels came for him in her car, for the bus trip to her home was a rather tiresome one.

"You're not only proving to be a friend in need," he said as they drove along, "but I'm having the pleasure of being with a very good driver," he added as she wound in and out of the heavy traffic.

"Thanks," she said. "I had instructions, but I had to get

confidence the hard way. Mother was brave enough to trust herself to me when I began to drive and I did have to be careful."

The church which Helen and her parents attended was no different from many other churches. The building was costly and beautiful, the choir was attractively robed and the anthems were quite melodious. The soloist had a beautiful voice with surprising volume, all of which Dick enjoyed, for he loved good music. When the minister began his sermon his interest waned and he sat there bored and hoping that it would soon be finished. There was nothing inspiring in what the man said. He began with a verse from some prophet with whom Dick wasn't familiar and then he gave a dissertation on the passage that contained the word "maybe." Maybe God would bring success to an undertaking, or in some work for Him when the odds seemed against it. Maybe this would succeed because God was in it. This was the whole discourse, for Dick didn't think it was much of a sermon. There was a defeatist attitude throughout the whole discourse.

"What did you think of the sermon?" Mr. Daniels asked on their way home.

"Well, I scarcely know what to say," Dick replied hesitatingly. "It seemed to me that he wasn't counting very strongly on the promises of God. That word 'maybe' seemed to dominate his thinking."

Dick felt like a hypocrite speaking about a faith which he didn't have himself.

"That was what I thought," Helen said. "I don't think he was at his best today. In fact, I don't think he'll ever measure up to Dr. Sanstrom." She turned to Dick. "He was our former pastor, but he died very suddenly and we have this one on probation. I don't think I would vote for him as our regular pastor, if I had a vote."

Mrs. Daniels remarked to Dick, "You talk as if you must have had a good minister in the church you attended back home. I wonder if you are a believer."

"I'll have to confess that I'm not," Dick replied. "My

mother is a Christian and it's not her fault that I'm not."

"I'm sure that she has been praying that one day you would be a believer, just as she is," she told him.

"I know that she has," he agreed, feeling guilty that he couldn't tell her that he was a believer.

After this he was a frequent visitor at the Daniels home and he enjoyed his association with these people, even though he did sometimes feel uncomfortable when they talked about the Lord. It made him think of his mother, for they repeated so many of the little things that she so often talked about, the Lord's blessings, the answer to prayers, and their hope and faith in Him. He missed his mother and was glad it would not be long before he could be with her again. He hadn't realized how dear she was and how large a part of his life she had filled, until he was away from her. Before he had just accepted her, but, now that he was away from her, he knew what a blessing she had been to him practically all of his life.

Another thing he had taken for granted before, was the happy home life he had had. It could have been so different. But even with the knowledge of those blessings, there was no thought of thanking God for them. Nothing was farther from his mind than to thank God for anything.

Then something happened that made him even more bitter toward God, the God who had failed him in the past.

Just a few days before he was to leave for home, he received a telegram from his father. "Mother very ill — come home at once."

Dick took the telegram to his superior and received permission to leave.

On the way home he sat rigid and tense as the plane rushed through the night. For the first time since he had stopped praying long ago, he kept repeating words to the God he had ignored all this long time.

"God! Don't let her die. Let me get there in time! Don't let her die!"

All through the long hours he kept repeating the same

words, but even while he repeated them, he did not actually feel the living reality of God. He was just repeating words, for God was not there. He was just Someone far, far away, whom he believed in, but who was not actually real to him. He did not realize that he didn't even have the right to pray and expect an answer, for that was reserved to those who belonged to God's family, those who had been born into it when they accepted salvation through the blood of Jesus Christ. God was Someone from whom he had cut himself away through the bitterness that had grown through the years, because his prayers had not been answered in the time and way that he wanted them answered.

Chapter Eighteen

Dick needed no sight of the flowers on the front door to tell him that he was too late, that his mother was dead. He had had a premonition before the plane landed.

When he entered the house he found it empty and he felt utterly forsaken and shaken. He couldn't remember a time in his early years when he had come home to an empty house.

His mother would be waiting to help him with his lessons if he needed help. When he had finished his home work and his studies, then he could go out and play. She explained that when a person is tired and sleepy, he couldn't do his best and she wanted him to be the best possible student.

Even when he was in college, she was seldom not there, for she wanted to be there to greet him when he came in and to give him a snack if he was hungry.

Not until recently had he realized what a sacrifice she had made for his comfort. Now she was no longer there. If he had been returning from some trip, if it was not possible for her to be at the station or airport to meet him, she would be at the door when the taxi drove up. And now she would never be there again to meet him and give him that motherly kiss and demonstration of her love.

The coldness and emptiness bore down upon him. He put his bags down and went into the living room and sat there where they had often sat on the couch. He buried his face in his hands and gave way to sobs that refused to be controlled.

Time passed, but he had no idea how long he had been there weeping out the agony of his loss until the front door opened and his father came in.

"Dick!" he cried. "I didn't expect you so soon. I had to be at the funeral home until just now to attend to everything."

Dick raised his tear-stained face and looked at his father. His father seemed to have aged since he last saw him. The man who had seemed so young and so alive when he had left, now looked his age and seemed to have lost all of his vitality. He looked pale and worn. Dick knew that sorrow had done this to him.

He came and sat beside Dick and for a time they said nothing, while Dick tried to control his tears.

"The house seemed so empty and forlorn when I came in," Dick remarked while his voice was still shaken with sobs. "It's almost the first time I ever came home and Mom didn't meet me. It seems more than I can stand."

"I know how you feel. Shouldn't I? We've been so close for so many years, long before you came to be with us. Now I feel like a ship lost at sea. I don't know where I shall turn or what I shall do. I just can't seem to face the future without her. Only the Lord can help me, for I need Him now more than I ever did."

Dick was silent, then he burst out," Why didn't the Lord let her live until I got here? He could have done that one little thing at least."

"I prayed that she would live until then," his father told him, "but the Lord knows best. I'm so glad that, long ago, she led me to the Lord, not so much by her words, though she did witness to me, but by her beautiful life. Even when I was sometimes cross and unreasonable when we were first married and before I had come to the Lord, she never would quarrel. She would just keep calm and silent until I was ashamed and would ask her to forgive me. She was saved right after we were married but I didn't have much faith in her salvation until I saw how she reacted when I would start a quarrel. It was after one of these outbursts, when I asked her forgiveness, that she said the thing that brought me to my knees. She said in the sweetest voice, 'Darling, you don't have to ask me for forgiveness. You need to ask God, because He alone can really forgive you and forget all your sin. I can't forget, but He has promised to remember them no more. Pray with me that when He has forgiven you, there need never be any more times like these between us.' I did what she asked me to do, to let us pray together, and I've been a changed man ever since."

His voice broke in a sob.

"Did she suffer any?" Dick asked when they could speak.

"No. She had a heart attack. She had had several little flare-ups but she never mentioned them to me, for she thought that I'd be worried and she didn't think that they were very serious. Her doctor didn't think that they were either."

"What a dumb doctor he was!" Dick ejaculated. "He should have warned you or me."

"No, he wasn't ignorant. In the first place, even the best of doctors can never predict too successfully about the heart. It sometimes plays out when it appears to be working perfectly. But he told me that she had asked him not to tell me anything about these little attacks. She didn't want to worry me needlessly. She wanted above everything that I should be happy and when you came along, she wanted that same thing for you."

"Didn't she even leave me a message?" Dick asked desperately. He felt that he could bear it a little better if he knew that she had left him some word.

"Not a message exactly, for she was unconscious for quite a while. Just before she died when she was under the oxygen, I saw her lips move and I leaned nearer so that I could hear what she was trying to say. She was calling your name, son."

"Did she say anything?" Dick asked tensely.

"I heard only a word or two. She was saying, 'Dick, Dick, please, please,' then in just a few minutes she was gone."

Tears began to fall again from Dick's eyes. His father put an arm around him and said in a voice shaken by sobs, "You know what she must have been trying to say. It must have been what was on her heart ever since the first day you came to us, that you would yield your heart to her Saviour. It was the one desire of her life for you. What better time than now, boy, to do that most important thing?"

Dick shook his head while he covered his face with his hands again and wept quietly, "I can't talk about it now," he said brokenly. "All I can think of is that she is gone and I'll never see her again."

"But you can have the blessed hope of seeing her again," his father insisted, "if you'll just ask God to forgive you and save you. You know the way, for you've heard it often enough, not only from her, but from our pastor. If you'll just trust Him, He will give you the comfort that I know He will bring to me in the days to come."

"How can I ask God to forgive me when I don't have any faith in Him? He failed me once and He's failed me again. I just can't do it."

"Oh, my boy! You're in such a dangerous state!" His father uttered a sigh that came from his broken heart.

He rose and remarked, "We'll go to the funeral parlor whenever you are ready. Rena will be coming soon to give us a little breakfast. Then we can go to her."

"I'm not hungry," Dick said.

"But you must eat to keep up your strength," his father insisted. "I don't feel hungry either, but I know that I'll have to carry on. There are so many things to do and so many arrangements to be made for the future. I'll have to keep on working and living somehow, for I'll have to carry on until the Lord takes me to her or else until He returns."

Dick went to his room to change and freshen up. He hated to go into his room which held so many memories of his mother. There on his dresser was his mother's photo taken with him on her lap when he was still a little fellow. He picked up the picture and looked at it for a long time. It was a good likeness of them both, but the expression upon her face as she looked down at him always assured him of her love. He had kissed the picture behind its glass many times and he kissed it reverently now as the tears flowed upon the glass.

Breakfast was just an attempt at eating. His father returned thanks as he had done through the years. When Rena came into the room with tears streaming down her face, they had a struggle to swallow a few bites.

"I hope you'll carry on for us, Rena," Richard said to her when she came in to clear off the table.

"I sure will," she said as her voice shook, "but it'll be as hard for me as it will for you, Mr. James."

"I know it, Rena, for you've been a part of the family for so long, and I know you loved her, too."

"She was a wonderful person," Rena said while the tears started again. "She never spoke one cross word to me, even when I was so new here and made so many mistakes. And she led me to the Lord. I'll thank her one day in glory for what I've thanked the Lord for all these years."

Something tore at Dick's heart. It was not grief for his mother, but he felt the gnawing pain and a longing that he could be like these two, that he could have the faith that they had, that he could have been obedient to his mother's pleadings. The enemy of man's soul kept alive within him the bitterness and the stubborn refusal to believe that it was for him. He didn't know that when he turned away from God and let his heart be hardened by unbelief, that he had laid himself open for the entrance of that enemy within his heart and that only through the Holy Spirit's power could that enemy be made to leave him free to accept the salvation that he had so long refused. He felt that he was an outcast, that God didn't want him and he let it go at that.

In this moment of agony, he almost wished that he had already come to the end of the road, for he had no desire to go on with his life.

He marveled at his father's quietly facing life, that he knew he must carry on, and he envied him his confident trust that God would take care of him and give him the strength to go on in His will.

Dick realized that he had no one but himself upon whom to lean and just now he felt more like just giving up and ending it all. He strove to master his grief as he joined his father and they left for the funeral home.

Nancy had been forgotten in his agony of grief and no thought of her intruded upon him as he went with his father to the quiet room where flowers were banked around the casket. He looked down upon the still form and the face so lovely and youthful in death, while silent sobs shook him. Then he followed his father into the small room at one side reserved for the family. He knew that he had looked upon his mother for the last time, that he would never see her again, either in this life and, if there was another after this, in the life which was to come.

It was when the brief service was over and they were coming out on their way to the waiting cars, that Dick saw Nancy and realized that for once she had been completely forgotten. In the brief moment when he saw her, he noticed that tears were streaming down her face. She was with some stranger, a rather tall man with dark hair and eyes. Dick observed in even that one glance that this stranger was quite good looking and that he seemed concerned about Nancy's tears. He whispered something to her, but it only made her tears come faster, so that she hid her face for a moment in her handkerchief.

While Dick waited for the car and then followed his father inside, even in that moment, the spirit of jealousy surged through him and for an instant he forgot his grief about his mother. This fellow must be in love with Nancy, but he had no right to her. She belonged to him. She should have been there beside him, trying to comfort him. Then he forgot her in the memory of where they were going, to put his mother away forever from his sight.

Dick wondered how he could carry on in the dark and lonely days ahead. He didn't want to carry on. What was the use? What was the use of anything? He would have to carry on and he would be carrying on in his own strength. The future held no ray of light. Dark clouds covered his sky, clouds of grief, unbelief and bitterness toward the only One who could have scattered those clouds and let the light of eternal life come in.

Chapter Nineteen

When Sunday came, Dick wondered what his father would want to do. He knew that he had never missed a church service when it was possible for him to be there. He was hoping that he wouldn't want to go, for he knew that he would be expected to go with him, but he felt that he just could not go.

His father asked Dick if he would go with him. When they came in to breakfast and Rena greeted them with a good morning, Dick saw that there were still traces of tears on her face. His father still looked pale and worn and so much older that it worried him.

When they had finished breakfast and sat together in the living room, each with a part of the paper, the loneliness and emptiness bore down upon Dick with crushing force. He wondered how his father could seem so much more cheerful than he himself was able to feel. It seemed to him that the end of the world had come, his world, at least.

When the time came for them to leave for church, his father turned to him and said, "You'll go to church with me, won't you?"

"Oh Dad! How can you want to go so soon afterward?" Dick cried. "Won't it seem strange to go so soon? People will think you don't care."

"Why should it seem strange?" his father wanted to know. "I would feel strange if I didn't go. I would be doing what-she-would want —" and his voice broke. "We never missed a service unless one of us was sick and that surely wasn't often. I'm thankful that God kept us well for so many years. It is only what I should do, go to the house of worship and continue to praise my God and my Saviour."

"Can you praise Him for taking Mother away when both of you could have had many years yet to be together?" Dick asked.

"Yes, I can. I can say like Job said so many years ago when God allowed Satan to take away everything, even his health. And his wife also tested his faith. He cried, 'The Lord gave and the Lord hath taken away, blessed be the name of the Lord.' That's what I can say today, Dick. I know that He did what He knew to be best and who am I to question what He did or why He did it? When you have that faith, son, tragedy can become a blessing, for God arranges it that way, if we trust Him."

Dick was silent, but his eyes were hard and there was a grim tenseness about his lips.

He didn't have the heart to refuse to go with his father, much as he dreaded the ordeal.

Pain tore at his heart again as he remembered the happy days when he was a little fellow sitting beside his mother and trying to understand what the preacher was saying, and failing completely.

He knew how hard it would be to sit there without her and he knew that the sermon would leave him cold, for he wouldn't even be listening but thinking of the past and dreading the future.

The ride to church was a heartbreaking experience for

both of them, but each reacted in a different way. Richard was praying for strength to endure the pain that filled his heart, while Dick was dreading the ordeal and feeling utterly forsaken, with no thought of turning to the Source of all strength. When they entered the building and approached the pew where they always sat, sympathetic eyes were turned upon them. Dick felt their gaze and it only made him more uncomfortable than ever.

Presently he saw Nancy enter and take her place in a pew to the right and in front of them. She was with the same stranger he had seen her with at the funeral. When the sermon began, he wasn't hearing a word. He was thinking of Nancy and the time when they had been together, when he had hope that she was beginning to care. He was thinking of the times when his lips and hers had met and she had responded to his kisses. And that agonizing time when she had told him that she could date him no longer.

Dick wondered if she had fallen in love with this stranger who seemed so attentive, or if she still loved him. He wished that he had refused to come this morning, for now he would be remembering what he was trying so hard to forget.

When the service was over, he saw Nancy looking at him, then she turned to her companion and said something. She was trying to make her way to him through those who were in her way. He didn't want to have to speak to her, so he hurried out before she could reach him.

He went to the car and unlocked it and sat inside waiting for his father. There were many who would be wanting to speak to his father and offer their sympathy. He didn't want that and he dreaded most of all to have Nancy offer her sympathy. It wasn't her sympathy he wanted, it was her love. Since he didn't have that, nothing else mattered.

"Why did you hurry out so fast?" his father asked when he joined him. "There were so many who wanted to speak to you. Everyone has been so kind to me. I appreciated what they said about your mother."

"I couldn't take it," Dick explained. "I couldn't stand it without making a baby of myself and I didn't want to do that."

"So many of them think so much of you. They like you and they can't forget that you were their hero on the football field." A little smile flitted across his father's face.

"That's been so long ago that I'd forgotten it," Dick replied.

They both went to work the next day. Dick was to report for work on his new job. His father remarked that it was good for them to have something to occupy their time, that it would be so much better than sitting around home and grieving. He was thankful that he could still carry on in his work.

Dick didn't feel thankful for anything. He dreaded starting at a new place where most of the workers would be strangers. Even though he felt that he had all the knowledge he needed to succeed at his new position, he dreaded having to make the necessary adjustments.

Mr. Stuart, the manager, greeted him cordially when he came and assigned him to his office and division. He spoke his sympathy and Dick thanked him. Then Dick was introduced to the other members of his department.

Dick knew a few of them and all of them remembered him from his football days. They reminded him of how they had cheered for him. What they said lifted him somewhat from his gloom and relieved his nervousness on this first day. Then the head of his department came in. He was the man who had been with Nancy.

"Forrest, I want you to meet a new member of the firm," Mr. Stuart said as he introduced them.

Dick tried not to betray his surprise as he responded to the introduction. Brad Forrest gave him a cordial greeting and said that he would be glad to have him join them. He offered to do anything he could to help Dick get adjusted.

"I wanted to meet you at church yesterday," he remarked as Mr. Stuart left them together, "but you hurried out so fast that I didn't get the opportunity. I didn't realize that you were the new member of this department until this morning. I do want to extend my sympathy for your loss. I know how terrible it must have been and what a shock to have it happen so suddenly and with you away. I can sympathize with you, for it happened just as suddenly to me when my mother died. I did have the good fortune to be with her, though, during those last few minutes."

Dick thanked him and agreed that it was pretty terrible, then began to ask a few questions about his work. He found it difficult to be pleasant to Brad Forrest, for he was already prejudiced against the man because of Nancy, but Brad was so friendly and so considerate as he explained the details of the routine, that Dick found it difficult to retain his resentment.

Dick wondered how he and Brad would get along, if anything came up, any mistake that he might make because of his present state of mind. As the day passed and he saw Brad's behavior and his friendly relation with the other men in his department, he felt ashamed of his attitude toward the man, even though he couldn't help it.

When closing time came he dreaded going back to that empty house which was no longer a home, just a shelter, for his father would not be coming in until later. He might just as well get used to it, he told himself, for this was what his life would be from now on.

When Sunday came again, he knew that he would be forced to go to church with his father, for he didn't have the heart to refuse him. When the announcements were made, it was mentioned that the new leader of the young adults would be presiding over their meeting next Sunday. The minister said how delighted they were to have Mr. Brad Forrest as their leader. He had been willing to take over when the former leader had been transferred and had to give up the class. The class would meet in their usual place and he invited every young adult to join the class for the lesson.

So this was the new leader and the new teacher, Dick thought. No wonder Nancy seemed interested in him. He was her kind, not an outcast whom she shouldn't love. She could enjoy his friendship and even accept his love, for it wouldn't be against her principles and there would be no fear of either of them being hurt by it.

Dick knew that it was foolish and childish to have such thoughts, but they still rankled within him. He knew that there was no reason why he should dislike Brad Forrest, for he was probably innocent and ignorant of any past relationship between himself and Nancy, but Dick disliked him anyway.

Though Dick had lost his opportunity to win Nancy because of his own stubbornness, he argued with himself in his defense, that it wasn't just stubbornness. It was something which he didn't seem to be able to conquer, something within him stronger than any desire to do what she had asked him to do. He couldn't pretend to be what he wasn't, no matter how much he wanted to please her and to win her. Some unseen power seemed to be holding him back whenever the desire stirred within him to become what she wanted him to be.

Chapter Twenty

Dick stood by the window staring out into space, but not really seeing what was before him. He held Nancy's little note of sympathy in his hands, for he had just finished reading it. It was like her, so warm and sympathetic, assuring him that she knew what he was suffering, for she had experienced the same deep sorrow. She was constantly in his thoughts. He couldn't help but be reminded of her because of her association with Brad Forrest. He tried to conquer his antagonism against Forrest, but it rose within him every time he came into contact with the man. Forrest must have come to the company with very high recommendations, he decided, to have them put him in such an important position. One of Dick's friends told him that Forrest had had experience elsewhere in this same line of work and that he was given this position in spite of his youth, when the former employee had been forced to retire because of ill health.

Nancy's note made him more unhappy than he had been when he faced the day ahead of him. Today was Saturday and there was no work at the plant. He faced a lonely day with little to occupy his time. His father was out playing golf. He had recently taken up the game and today he had advised Dick to come with him and have a little practice.

"It helps to pass a long day," he remarked. "How about it? I can be a good teacher, though I'm such a poor player."

Dick gave him a playful smile. "Thanks, Dad, but I'm not old enough to begin that sport."

His father chuckled at his remark, glad that Dick could at least smile again. It had been so long since he had seen a smile upon the young face.

"Don't be putting me with the ancients, young man," and he held up a warning finger. "I'm still in the younger bracket, even though I'm not as young as you are."

It had been raining during the night, but the sun had come out and the raindrops upon the leaves glimmered like bright jewels. Presently Dick's attention was attracted by the mournful cry of a cardinal sitting upon a branch nearby. He idly watched the bird for a moment, wondering why such a pitiful call. Surely the little fellow was calling for help, though he didn't seem to be in trouble. He sounded almost human as he sat there with his head held high so that the little tuft of feathers on his head pointed rakishly to the blue sky above. Dick wished that he could interpret bird language, if they had one, for there surely was heartbreak in that loud cry. Then presently he

thought he understood the cause of that cry, for from somewhere across the way a little female, with her dull brown
coloring and only a hint of red here and there upon her
small body, flew to him and landed on the branch beside
him. For a moment they sat there twittering in low tones,
then they flew down and began looking for seeds or in-
sects and they were twittering in the same low tones, just
like a happy human couple would do, contented to be
together.

He sighed and turned from the window. Pain surged
through him again with renewed strength. There would be
no such reunion for him, no working together in the happy
little tasks of life. That prospect was closed forever to him.

He realized that he was slowly but surely changing from
the happy, genial person he had been all through his life,
that he was becoming moody and grumpy and that bitterness was making him sour upon the whole world and toward
everyone in it. He defended himself by arguing that it
was not his fault that the change was coming, but that
it was life and people and — dared he say it? — God.

He forgot that God had made it possible for him to
have a happy home and two wonderful parents, when he
could have been placed in an orphanage where he would
never have known the love of parents. His parents had
done everything in their power for him, yet Dick had denied himself the one thing that was most important in life.
He had been denied that because he had refused to accept
it through his own stubborn will. They could not force
him to accept something against his will.

Dick sat down and thought over his life, realizing what
he had become and realizing that he was becoming more
morose as time passed. Still he had no desire to overcome
that trend, no desire to seek help from the only One who
could change him and make him what he once was, a child
with a faith in a God who was love.

When his father returned, tired but cheerful and eager
to talk about what had happened on the golf course, Dick
wondered how his father could be so cheerful when there

was nothing left in life but work and loneliness, growing older and finally ending it all in a coffin under the ground.

"You should have been there," his father said. "You should have seen that young fellow, no older than you, shoot a hole in one. Talk about an old man's game would you? That young man is headed for professional golfing, if I'm not greatly mistaken." As Dick made no comment, but sat there listening respectfully, but unsmiling, the picture of gloom, his father asked, "Dick, what's the matter? What's on your mind?"

"I was just wondering how you could forget Mother so soon," he replied accusingly.

"Forget her! Are you out of your mind? How could I forget her when she's been a part of my life for so long? What do you expect me to do? Sit at home and mope as you're doing? I'd feel ashamed of myself if I did."

"Then I suppose you're ashamed of me," Dick remarked sourly.

"If you want the truth, I am," his father admitted. "My heart aches so that I can scarcely keep back the tears sometimes, even at work, I try not to let it keep me down. If I'm really trusting the Lord to help me to carry on and live in the hope of His return, I've got to do my part. I can at least try to be cheerful, even though I sometimes feel more like crying. And I can still do something for my Lord. Just today I had the opportunity to talk to one of the men at the club when they got to talking about the condition of the world today. I told him what the Bible says about this and how prophecy is being fulfilled. One of the other fellows was so interested that he said he wanted to hear more about this and I have a date to visit him next week so that his wife can hear what I was talking about. That's the way a Christian should live, Dick. Not to mope, but to try to carry on as God leads the way."

"I'm afraid I don't have any leading," Dick remarked as a sigh escaped him.

"It's because you turned your back on the Leader," his father told him. "Somewhere along the way you've turned your back on God. I don't know how or why you did it, but I know that it grieved your mother and it worried me. You'll never have real peace in your heart until you find the way back and only God can lead you. Think it over," he advised.

When Sunday came again, Dick knew that he would go with his father to church, much as he disliked to go, and he knew that he would sit there thinking of everything but what the preacher was saying. He hoped that he wouldn't see Nancy and Brad Forrest together, but there they were when he entered the church, sitting in the same place, side by side.

When the Superintendant of the Sunday school made the announcement about the young adult class, he said a few words that made Dick suddenly listen with interest. He asked Nancy to stand up and Nancy, looking very much embarrassed, obeyed.

"I want to introduce Miss Nancy Crawford whom many of you know already. She has been elected as assistant teacher to Mr. Brad Forrest. I'm sure that with both of them working together, our young people will grow even more interested than they have been. Everyone of you here this morning are cordially invited to attend the class next Sunday morning. Miss Crawford will be teaching in the forced absence of Mr. Forrest on business."

Dick heard even less of the sermon after that. If he had been listening with an open heart and mind, perhaps he would have heard what he needed, for the sermon was based on the familiar story of the Good Shepherd who went out into the desert to find the one lost sheep. Dick's father was praying earnestly that Dick would listen with his heart and that he as the one lost sheep would follow the Shepherd to the fold, but his prayer was not answered in the way and the time that he had hoped for, for when they left he could see by the expression upon Dick's face that the sermon had left him cold.

Dick was thinking of Nancy and Brad Forrest. He wondered if they were engaged and if they were, how soon their engagement would be announced. He was sure that they were in love.

Chapter Twenty-One

Dick wondered what kind of a teacher Nancy would be. He knew that she had all the qualifications to hold attention as far as beauty and personality, and he was sure that she knew her Bible better than many of those who would be under her ministry. She would inspire her hearers by her supreme faith in God and her love for Him. He knew the courage it took for her to cut herself off from him if she really loved him, and she never would have confessed her love if she had not loved him. He knew her capacity for love for others, for he had seen that demonstrated in the little incident with the old woman.

He wished that he could attend her class, but of course he knew that he dared not. Every time he saw her, the pain was renewed. It seemed that it would always be with him to torment him.

He had no interest in any other girl, consequently he had no desire to try to date any of them. He had left that foolish attempt to go the limit and play the field as Scott had suggested. Now he was rapidly becoming a recluse.

His father urged him to go out and mingle with people.

"You'll never be able to enjoy life as you should, if you don't get out of this house and be with people. I'd go crazy if I sat around and moped as you're doing. You'll grow sour and moody, old before your time. Don't you care anything for people?"

He shrugged. "Who is there to care for beside you?" Dick asked.

"I'm sure you know lots of interesting people your age. Why not renew your friendship with them?" he urged. "It isn't natural for you to sit here alone like this and either read or mope and watch those rotten shows on TV. I want you to marry some nice girl and be happy again. You'll never have the opportunity to fall in love with someone, if you don't get out and meet them."

"I don't want to fall in love," Dick replied morosely. "I did that once and that's enough for me. I don't want another try at it."

"You mean Nancy?" his father asked.

Dick nodded.

"I thought you two were hitting it off and I was sorry when it fell through. Did you have a quarrel? I'm sure that she thought a lot of you. I noticed her crying at the funeral."

Dick was glad that his mother had never told his father what had happened between Nancy and himself.

"Let's not talk about it, Dad, please. That's all over and for good. I don't want to go through with anything like that again. Please give me time and perhaps I can snap out of this low into which I've sunk. I'll try for your sake. You're carrying on so well. You're becoming a gad-about. You're almost out every night."

"I'm not out gadding," his father informed him gravely. "Every night I've been out I have been on the Lord's business. I'm not going out just to forget. I never can forget, but I know that the Lord wants me to work for Him as long as I'm able and that's what I've been doing. When your mother was alive, perhaps I was too well satisfied just to spend my evenings with her. Life was so complete with her — and with you, my son."

He gave Dick a tender smile that brought the sting of tears to Dick's eyes.

"You remember the man I told you about, who wanted me to come to his house and tell him and his wife what I had talked about at the club? Well, I went there last night and before I left, both that man and his wife accepted the Lord and were redeemed from their sin. It was so wonderful that I still thank the Lord for that joy. I hope to spend the rest of my life trying to win souls. There is no greater joy than winning a soul."

"Where to tonight?" Dick asked as he saw that his father was going out.

"I'm going to see some people from the church who haven't been attending for a long time. I want to see if I can find out why they're not coming. I may be able to help them in some way, or even win them if they're not saved."

"Let me wish you success," Dick offered.

"I only wish that I could have success, as you call it, with you, my son. I'd give my life if I could win you for the Lord."

Pain shot through Dick's heart at the words. They were the same that his mother had spoken in the past that seemed part of another age. He remembered his mother's last words, that last "please" that she had uttered as her last breath had left her.

"Just keep on praying, Dad. Perhaps one day your prodigal son will come home." He smiled faintly, trying to assume a more cheerful attitude.

When his father left, he turned on the TV but there was nothing that interested him and he turned it off. It was true. The shows were getting more and more ordinary and uninteresting.

Just before Brad Forrest left on a short business trip, he spoke to Dick.

"I wish you would come to our young adult class. I'm sure you'll like Nancy's teaching. She has such a wonderful personality and she's so dedicated. I wanted her to be the permanent teacher, but she refused. She said that a man should be the teacher, so I'm stuck. I couldn't invite you out to hear me, with much enthusiasm, but I can urge you to come and hear her."

Dick knew that it was foolish, but cold anger swept over him at the casual way he mentioned Nancy's name. He no longer had any claim upon her and Brad had every right to whatever relationship might be between them and to enjoy that relationship. That knowledge didn't make Dick any less resentful, however.

His voice sounded coldly polite as he replied. "Thanks, but I'm not interested."

Brad gave him a long, searching glance before he spoke again.

"Please tell me why you dislike me so much?"

"What makes you think that?" Dick asked, amazed that Brad should have guessed the truth. He had not dreamed that it had been so plainly revealed.

"I can see it in your every expression, feel it in the tone of your voice, in everything that you say, even though you're so careful to be polite. What have I done to merit your dislike?"

"You haven't done anything," Dick confessed, feeling ashamed of himself. "I'm sorry if I haven't been polite."

"You've been polite, too polite," Brad told him. "I'm sorry you feel as you do. I wanted to be friends."

"I'm sure you're mistaken about me," Dick denied defensively.

"I'm sure I'm not," Brad contradicted, "but let's forget it." As he turned toward the door he said, "I'll be leaving in a few minutes, so try not to miss me too much." He gave Dick a smile and was gone.

Dick wondered whether he was trying to be sarcastic or whether he was just joking. Neither thought made him any happier.

It was cold and windy, with low hanging clouds that made it seem even colder. When his father went out to play golf at the weekend, Dick urged him not to go, but he insisted that the exercise would keep him warm and that he would stay out of the rain if it came.

There was no rain, but it grew colder, with dampness that made it even more penetrating. When his father came in later than usual he shivered and wrapped his bathrobe around him while they waited for dinner to be served. The room was too warm for Dick and he was worried about his father. It wasn't usual for him to be so cold in such a heated room.

He drank a couple of cups of coffee, but ate very little and he went to his room soon after dinner, complaining that he was very tired. Dick was more worried, for his father never seemed to tire even after a long round of golf. It must have been well after midnight when he heard his father call faintly from his room.

"Dick, will you please phone for Dr. Madden? I think I have a chill."

Dick was now thoroughly frightened and phoned the doctor at once. He was there very soon and Dick took him at once to see his father. He stood by nervously waiting while the doctor took the sick man's temperature, then took his blood pressure and took out his stethescope. His father was now gasping for breath and was showing that he was in intense pain.

"Pleural pneumonia," the doctor told Dick in low tones. "He should be taken to the hospital immediately."

Dick phoned for an ambulance and soon his father was on his way to the hospital with Dick sitting beside him, frightened and nervous.

The doctor followed in his car and Richard was put in a private room with nurses engaged. Dick sat through the rest of the night, in spite of his father's plea for him to get some rest.

"I'll be all right with the nurse and with the Lord," he told Dick.

"How could I rest when you're here so sick and suffering?" Dick asked. "My place is here and it's where I want to be, so please rest quietly and get well soon."

Before long Richard was put under an oxygen tent and was gasping for his life. Dick sat there tense with terror. He would be so utterly alone if his father died. They had grown closer together since they had been alone, in spite of the differences in their outlook on life. Dick felt that he wouldn't be able to go on without him. He was so tired that he could scarcely sit up, but he couldn't leave until finally his father drifted into a troubled sleep. He didn't know that it was not a natural sleep, but one induced by a strong sedative, but he did know by the doctor's grave face that his father was in very serious condition.

Finally when night came again, he was persuaded to go home when the nurse promised to call him if there was any change in his father's condition.

As the taxi sped through the darkness, Dick had the same feeling that he'd had about his mother, that he would lose his father also. Then he would really be alone, left once more as he had been when he was a little tot. Left alone in a world in which there was no place to turn. This time there would be no foster mother or father to take him in and make life livable and happy again. There would be no place to turn, no one who could help him to carry on as his father had tried to help him to do.

He had no heavenly Father to whom to turn in this hour of such desperate need, for he had banished Him even from his thoughts.

The night was dark and the horizon of his life was even darker.

Chapter Twenty-Two

Dick was wakened from the sleep of exhaustion by the ringing of the telephone. He knew what it was before he heard the voice of the nurse telling him that he had better come because his father wasn't doing so well. She told him that an intern was with him and that the doctor was on his way.

He threw his clothes on and drove down the silent streets, breaking every traffic law, his only thought to get there before it was too late. He waited impatiently for the elevator and was on the point of running up the three flights of steps when it finally came. When he reached the third floor he could hear his father's labored breathing and he uttered a sigh of relief as he ran down the hall and entered the room. The nurse and the intern were there near the bedside.

Dick went to his father's side and called his name in low tones. The dying man opened his eyes, looked at Dick and smiled feebly, then tried to speak. Dick could scarcely hear the gasping, whispered words.

"I prayed for you before I passed out." He stopped because he didn't have the strength to go on.

Just then the doctor came. Richard's eyes were closed and his breath was becoming weaker with every effort. The doctor needed no examination to tell him that his patient was going fast.

Dick stood at the foot of the bed while his heart responded in torturing throbbing that accompanied the weakening breathing of the one lying there who had meant so much to his own life.

Suddenly Richard opened his eyes and looked at Dick standing there silent and stricken. His lips moved and Dick could barely hear the few words he tried to utter. He understood more by the movement of his father's lips than by the sound that was so feeble.

"Dick, please, please accept —" then the feeble efforts failed and Richard's soul had gone to meet the Lord whom he had worshiped and tried to serve.

Dick stood petrified, unable to move or think.

The doctor saw and understood. "Would you like for us to take care of everything?" he asked.

Dick looked helplessly at the doctor and nodded, then turned to the nurse.

"I'll send you a check tomorrow," he told her. "I believe your time was up last night."

"Don't worry about that," she told him. "We'll take care of everything. You go home and try to get some rest."

He thanked her mechanically and tried to thank the

doctor, but his voice failed him and after a moment he turned and walked with leaden feet to the elevator.

Despair surged through him in great waves. He had led such a protected life and had depended upon both parents for comfort and advice, and even with his father in the short while that they had been together alone, he had never really been on his own. Now he was completely on his own. He was adrift — utterly alone. There was no one to whom he could turn for comfort or companionship. Life would be even more empty than when his mother had died. He dreaded more than ever the thought of going on alone, though he knew that he would have to, but there would be no purpose or desire in the life that faced him in the future.

His father's pastor came to the house as soon as he learned of Richard's death. He had gone to the hospital the evening before and he knew how little hope there was for his faithful member.

He talked for a while with Dick and discussed the simple funeral arrangements that Dick wanted. Dick finally agreed that a service should be conducted in the church, though he did not want it. But the pastor convinced him that his father's friends would want to be there, for there were many who would want to pay him this last tribute.

The pastor knew that Dick wasn't a Christian and he longed to say something that might break down his bitter wall of resistance to the whisper of the Holy Spirit, but he felt that this might not be the time to speak. He couldn't leave, however, without saying some little word that might help to make Dick realize what he was missing by not trusting the Lord.

"I pray that you will find comfort from the same source that your father found in his hour of sorrow," he said. "I know that was the one thing that both of your parents wanted more than anything else, that you would yield your life to the Saviour who died that you might have eternal life."

"I didn't know that my parents had discussed such intimate facts with an outsider," Dick remarked coldly.

"Only because they loved you and they wanted me to join them in prayer that their greatest desire for you might be met. I have done that ever since they asked me to join them," he replied.

"Thanks, but I'd rather not discuss it," Dick said.

The pastor knew that he had said all that he could, so after again repeating his sympathy and telling Dick how much he had been helped by his parents and how much he had been encouraged by them when he came to the church as a young pastor, he left. Even more than by the death of his faithful church member, he was saddened by the knowledge of Dick's bitter rebellion against God. He could only continue to pray that in His own time the Lord would answer the prayer of years by Dick's parents.

Dick sat as immobile as a statue carved from granite during the short service at the church. Though he sat so quietly, no one knew that he was exerting every effort within him against crying out in agony because of the pain within him.

As he came out of the church, he met Nancy who was waiting for him, but he scarcely noticed her. She was just a blur that he saw out of the corner of his eye, a blur that mingled with the others who were waiting as he slowly followed his father's casket to the waiting car.

As he passed her, she put her hand on his arm and whispered, "Dick, how my heart aches for you! Please believe me. I know how much you loved him. I know just how you feel, for I've had that same sorrow."

Her voice failed, choked by a sob. Dick thanked her mechanically and quickened his step. He didn't want to be stopped by any others offering sympathy. What could anyone do to help him? Not by words of sympathy. He was in the pit of despair and no human effort could help.

His rebellious heart cried out in bitter accusation. "God! God! Why did this have to happen? Haven't You done enough? Couldn't You have left him at least for a little while longer?"

Scalding tears ran unheeded down his face. Not even a

tinge of fear invaded his thoughts at this outcry. It was a cry that many others had uttered, lost souls who refused to believe that there was love even in tragedy, if there was faith to believe it.

When Sunday came he didn't even consider going to church. He had entered that door for the last time, he decided. There would be no obligation to anyone to keep going in order not to hurt them. He never considered that it would hurt the One who had died for him, that His blood had been shed for him in order that he might have the strength to go on as his father had done, with peace in his heart and hope for the future.

Dick entered doggedly into his work, working overtime when there was no need for it, sitting at his desk until he was too weary even to think straight and then going home and dropping off to sleep, hoping for forgetfulness. He was striving not to think, but it seemed that the more he tried, the more insistent these troubling, agonizing thoughts became. If he had been used to drinking, he probably would have become a confirmed alcoholic, but he had never had the taste of liquor in his home and had never acquired the custom of drinking even at parties where liquor was served.

Brad Forrest saw what was happening to Dick and he was afraid that if something didn't happen to deliver him from this dangerous mental state, he would crack up. He was concerned about Dick's soul, but he was afraid to speak to Dick about his soul, for Dick had manifested his dislike so plainly that he realized it might make Dick resentful if he said anything.

If he hadn't been a consecrated Christian, he would have resented Dick's attitude and would have retaliated by making it difficult for Dick in his work.

He prayed for guidance and he finally decided to speak to Dick, no matter what the consequences might be. He came into the office where Dick was bent over his work, though all the others had left.

"You can't keep this up, fella, or you'll break down," he began. "There's no need of your working so late, even though we are pushed for time. You'll get sick and then where will we be? You've become a vital part of this work and all of us realize how valuable you've become. For our sakes as well as your own, take more time off and get more rest."

"Thanks for the advice, but I'm better satisfied here than anywhere else," Dick replied. "It keeps me from thinking and I don't want to think. I don't want time to think."

"I know how you feel, for I've been along that same road," Brad told him. "I had almost passed beyond the point of no return when the Lord was merciful and I've lived to thank Him every day since then for giving me peace, no matter what life might bring to me. You can have that same peace that I have, if you'll only do what I did."

"And what was that?" Dick asked without any real interest. He didn't want to hear the answer, but he had to be polite, even if he wasn't interested.

"It's a long story, but I hope it won't bore you. My parents were not Christians and I never knew much about God until after they died. My father died first and my mother was as bitter as you are now, until one day she talked to a young girl who had met her at my father's grave. That young girl had just lost her mother, but she had such peace in spite of her sorrow. Then she began to talk to my mother and to explain the Source of that peace. When my mother left that cemetery, she had that same peace in her heart, for she had accepted Christ as her Saviour. When my mother came home she told me what had happened. I wasn't interested at the time and it wasn't until after my mother died that I finally realized that I needed what my mother had found. I was just as bitter as you are now and just as lost in a fog of despair, but since I came to the Lord and received His salvation through Jesus Christ, my whole life has been different. I have peace in my heart and hope for the future. You can have that same peace if you'll do what I had to do, for what God did for me, He'll do for you."

"Thanks for telling me," Dick said in that same cold, indifferent voice, "but I'm afraid I can't accept as you have done. Perhaps I've gone too far down that road. I want peace, of course, but I'm afraid I'll never find it in the way you did."

"I shall pray that you will," Brad said quietly as he left.

When Dick finally left and drove home, he was thinking of what Brad had said. How wonderful to have peace instead of bitterness and despair in his heart. Perhaps some day he might be able to find it, he mused, then he dismissed it from his mind. He resolutely closed his mind to any further thinking about it, for it only made him more miserable. He went to bed as soon as he could get there and tried to go to sleep without thinking, trying to keep his mind a complete blank, something that he found it impossible to do.

Brad went to his knees when he left Dick and prayed earnestly that somehow, some way, in God's time, Dick would yield to the voice of the Holy Spirit and receive salvation before it was too late.

He recalled a passage in his Bible that read, "He that being often reproved, and hardeneth his neck, shall suddenly be destroyed and that without remedy." He prayed that Dick would not wait until that day came. He prayed that if it was the Lord's will, he might be the means of leading him to the Lord.

Brad knew that God did not always answer prayer in the time and manner that man hoped and planned for and he was willing to wait. One day he was going to be made aware of that fact. And that day was not long in coming.

Chapter Twenty-three

The weeks passed slowly as time dragged on for Dick. The darkness that had descended upon his life and within him did not seem to grow less. He still worked with such intensity that his friends in the office wondered how long he could endure the strain.

Brad said nothing more to him, but he prayed earnestly that in some way he might speak to Dick and help him to climb out of this pit of despair, for it was written upon his face so clearly. He saw it and knew the reason, though the others might not know.

Dick was friendly to those in his department, but he never engaged in conversation with them except when something came up about the work. He never joined them in their coffee breaks nor at lunch. Most of them ate in the company cafeteria, but Dick ate at a lunch counter nearby. Though they noticed this, they didn't criticize him for being so unfriendly. They knew how deeply his grief affected him, though they realized that it was taking an unusually long time for him to recover from it.

Nancy had hoped that Brad might be able to persuade Dick to come to their class, for she knew how lonely he was. But though she prayed about it, it seemed that God was not going to answer her prayers in the way and time that she hoped for.

One day she spoke to Brad about this and asked him how Dick was getting along with his work.

"He's down in the depths and doesn't seem to have the desire to make the effort to snap out of it," Brad told her. "He's killing himself working. Isn't there something that you could say that might help him? You said that you had known him for a long time."

"I've tried to talk to him about the Lord, but he wasn't interested," she told him. "I keep praying for him because I know that his parents prayed and hoped that he would be saved while they were still living."

Brad wondered if there had been something more than friendship between these two. Dick's attitude distressed him. He couldn't understand how a boy who had had such Christian training in a home where both parents were Christians, could be so bitter and so antagonistic toward the mention of salvation. Surely there was something terribly wrong beneath the surface that was responsible for this. But he knew that nothing was impossible with God and he continued to pray. He remembered the passage in Proverbs that promised that if a child was brought up in the right way, when he was old he would not depart from it and he knew that God was faithful to keep His word. But he wondered how long it would take.

Late one afternoon, when everyone but Dick was preparing to leave for the day, they heard what sounded like an explosion in the basement. It didn't cause any concern that it might be one, until those on the second floor saw smoke seeping through underneath the closed door. When they opened the door, smoke swirled in from the floor below, brought in by the updraft along the stairway.

They all fled in panic to the street below while presently those on the floor above became aware of the fire somewhere below and they also rushed down the stairs and into the street, coughing from the smoke.

Dick was on the phone about an order that had not come through and he had his back to the door and didn't notice that the others had left. He had heard the loud voices of the others as they fled, but they so often were noisy when they went out together, that he paid no attention to it. He didn't see the black whirling mass coming through the half-open door until he hung up and turned back to his desk. He closed his desk and fled from the room, for he knew that somewhere below a fire was raging. Even in his haste he realized that some strong chemical must have been used to cause the fire or there wouldn't be such a volume of terribly black smoke. The fumes were so strong that he almost strangled as he went out into the hall and he was almost blinded so that he started the wrong way for the stairway. Then he remembered the important papers upon which he had spent so many hours working. He must get those papers, he decided, though he knew that it would only delay him and might prevent him from getting outside safely. Putting his handkerchief over his mouth and nose, he stumbled blindly in the direction of his office. He opened the drawer of his desk and grabbed up what he hoped was all of those papers. He jammed them into his pocket and again started for the stairway. This time he went in the right direction and began to run down the stairs. He lost his footing, stumbled and rolled over and over down the steps. He was already weakened by the smoke he had inhaled and by the time he reached the bottom of the stairway, he had lost consciousness.

In the meantime someone had phoned for the fire department and the employees were milling about outside, in excited groups, saying how fortunate they were to have gotten out in time.

Brad looked over the group, trying to see if everyone was there. Then he called to them to stop their noise and answer him.

"Are you sure that everyone is out of there?" he asked.

Silence followed his question as everyone looked around trying to see if they were all there.

"Line up over there," Brad cried, "and each of you call out your name and be quick about it."

Obediently the fifteen or twenty men lined up and called their names. Then Brad knew that Dick was missing.

"Where is Dick James?" he called. "Has anyone seen him?"

"He was on the phone when we all ran out of our offices," one of the men said. "We thought, of course, that he was following. We never thought of anything but getting out of there."

Brad pulled out his handkerchief and wet it at a hydrant nearby and started toward the door as he put it over his nose and mouth.

"Don't try to go in there," one of the men shouted while another caught hold of him and tried to hold him. "You'll die if you go in there! By this time that building is an inferno."

"I've got to go if there's a chance of saving him," Brad

said jerking loose. "He'll die and he's not ready to die. He's not saved."

He rushed inside and was lost to their sight.

"What did he mean by that?" one of the men asked as they all drew nearer the smoking building. They didn't expect to see Brad again. They were sure that he had gone to his death.

As Brad entered the building, he was almost blinded by the smoke. Tears began to fill his eyes. He began to choke from the acrid fumes, for his wet handkerchief was a poor mask. This fire had not been caused by natural means. Brad feared that he'd never make it to the floor where Dick's office was and his only hope was that Dick was able to get outside and come below. He kept doggedly on, determined to do everything in his power to save the one for whom he had been praying so earnestly. The thought appalled him as he struggled on, gasping for breath. If Dick died, he would go out into a Christless eternity.

As he stumbled on in the semi-darkness, fearing that he couldn't go much further or he would be overcome by the smoke, the memory of a verse came to him from the gospel of John, "Greater love hath no man than this, that a man lay down his life for his friends."

He prayed as he crept along, becoming weaker, "Lord, I'm willing to die, but let me save him. He's not ready to die."

It seemed ages since he had entered that building, but in reality it had been only a few minutes. But he was almost on the point of blacking out as the smoke was seeping into his lungs.

When he was wondering if he could go on or give up without finding Dick, he thought he saw the outline of something at the foot of the stairs. As he drew nearer, gasping for breath, he saw that it was Dick. He tried to raise him and drag him toward the door, hoping to be able to call for help when he reached the door. But he felt his strength failing and knew that he would not get far for he was losing consciousness. He made one last supreme effort and dragged Dick's body a little ways. The last thing he knew was the wail of the sirens as the fire department drew near. Firemen entered a moment after he fell and took both men out into the open air.

It took only a little while for those experts in handling such cases to restore Brad to consciousness, but Dick was still unconscious and as still as if he were already dead.

Presently an ambulance that had been summoned drew up and both men were placed inside and driven to a nearby hospital. They were put in the same room while a doctor and a nurse came to take care of them, followed by an orderly with a respirator.

Brad lay there slowly recovering after he had been attended to and he waited nervously for some sign of life from the unconscious Dick. After a time, the doctor shook his head.

"If he doesn't react soon, he'll be past hope," he remarked to Brad.

Presently Dick began to breathe in short shuddering gasps while Brad uttered a prayer of thanksgiving.

"When he had begun to breathe naturally, the nurse removed his coat so that he could rest more comfortably. As she did so, papers fell out of his pocket. She turned to Brad and handed them to him.

"Is this of any importance?" she asked.

Brad took the crumpled papers and glanced at them.

"I should say that they are important," he told her. Then to himself, "He must have gone back for this. Faithful even unto death, even if he was so indifferent to anything pertaining to God. Lord, give me one more chance to talk to him and let this be the time when he will break down and come to Thee. Let me make him realize how near death he was and that he wasn't ready for it."

With this prayer on his lips he lay back and went to sleep. He was exhausted and still weak, but he hadn't thought of himself and his own narrow escape from death.

Chapter Twenty-four

Brad was awake early. Fully recovered from his ordeal, he knew that there was much to be done at the plant. He sat on the side of the bed and looked across at Dick. The other was very pale and Brad realized what a narrow escape he'd had. He hoped that there had not been any damage to Dick's lungs. He wished that while they were there alone, he could have another talk with Dick. Perhaps this time he would be willing to listen when he realized his narrow escape.

While he sat looking meditatively at Dick and praying that the Lord would use him to win this soul of the one who had been such a burden upon his heart, Dick opened his eyes.

"Where am I?" he asked as he stared at Brad.

"You're in the hospital. Remember, you were overcome by smoke and you were just rescued in time. I thank God for that."

"Who did it?" Dick asked.

"I tried," Brad confessed," but the firemen really saved you." He was silent for a moment, then remarked, "I thank God that we got to you in time."

Dick didn't answer. Brad leaned over him, wanting to say something and waiting for help to decide what to say, as he was kept silent. Dick was staring at him with wide eyes, fixed as if he were hypnotized. His mouth flew open and he looked as if he saw something that paralyzed him so that he couldn't speak.

"What's the matter?" Brad asked, wondering what had happened. There was such a look of incredulity and perhaps of terror on Dick's face and in his eyes.

Dick pointed to Brad's neck. His shirt was open at the throat.

"That scar!" Dick cried in a hoarse whisper. "How did you get it?"

Brad put his hand over the scar and gave Dick a smile.

"It's not a very pretty sight and I don't blame you for looking like that when you saw it. I usually try to keep it hidden. Pride, you know. Such a handsome fellow as I am shouldn't have such a disfiguring mark on him. Sorry it's upset you so."

"How did you get it?" Dick persisted, still staring with wide eyes at the scar.

"It happened years ago. My brother gave it to me when we were little kids. I used to show it to the other kids, for I was proud of it. But I've learned better now. I got it in a game my brother and I were playing."

Dick gasped and sudden tears blinded him. He struggled to speak, but for a moment he couldn't. Emotion overwhelmed him and kept him speechless.

"Ted!" he finally gasped. "Is it you? But it can't be! Tell me, is it you?"

Brad uttered a cry of amazement and this time it was he who couldn't speak. He stared at Dick in unbelief, then he exclaimed, "Tag!" He stared a moment longer while he searched Dick's face for some sign of resemblance to the little fellow he once had been.

"Nobody living knows that name but you!" he exclaimed, "Yet it's so unbelievable."

He knelt by the bed and again searched Dick's face, then he murmured, "They told me that you were dead," and his voice broke.

"I tried to find you and I prayed that God would let me find you," Dick told him. "My mother told me that God would always answer those who trusted Him and believed that He would answer prayer. She told me that if I asked Him, he would keep His promise to let me find you. But He never did and I grew so bitter that I almost hated Him." A note of sadness entered his voice.

"But He did, Tag, He did," Brad told him. "You've found me at last. He did let you find me. We've found each other at last."

"But why did He wait so long?" Dick asked. "I needed you when I was praying for you then. Why did He keep me waiting all these years when I needed you so back there? I was so heartbroken without you. At last I stopped praying and I stopped believing."

"Then you became bitter and angry with God," Brad stated. He put an arm around Dick. "And you refused to believe Him or His Word. Is that what happened?"

Dick nodded. "Why did He wait so long? When I was so lonely and so miserable, when I couldn't tell anyone because I knew that they couldn't help me. Only God could and He didn't."

"But God took His own time and He answered your prayer in the best way," Brad explained. "If I hadn't been there at just the right time to save you, you would have died a horrible death, for no one else was willing to go into that blazing building. Now I know why I had such a burden on my heart for your soul and why I had to try to save you, even if I should die in the attempt. I knew that you were not ready to die, Tag. I've prayed for you ever since I first met you. Now I know why."

"But if I had found you years ago when I prayed, then perhaps I might have been ready to die instead of being so bitter. Why was that?"

The old doubt was still there, reluctant to yield.

"I don't know, Tag, I only know that God answers prayer in His own time and in His own way. We can't question Him, we just have to believe and wait. Just be glad as I am that we've found each other and that we need never be separated again."

"You said they told you that I was dead," Dick remarked. "Why did they do that?"

"When my foster parents first took me, I wouldn't eat and I cried so much that I was actually ill. They tried to find you, but you had moved away and then they told me that you were dead. They seemed to think that if I knew that, I would stop grieving because you were somewhere where I couldn't find you. You know the rest of the story. I don't suppose my mother ever thought that it would be right to tell me the truth about you. I don't hold that against her, for she was so good to me and I was happy with her and my father even though they were not Christians. You were fortunate enough to have Christian parents. You should thank God for them."

"I suppose I should," Dick admitted.

"Don't you think this would be a good time to thank God for bringing us together even after all this time?" Brad asked as he stroked Dick's forehead as if he were still a little child.

"I'm afraid He wouldn't hear me if I did after all this time," Dick said rather mournfully. "I don't have the right even to thank Him, for I've almost hated Him for so long."

"You can have that right, Tag," Brad said tenderly. "If you'll just ask Him to forgive you for every wrong thought and rebellious refusal to accept the salvation that He has been ready to offer you all this time."

"I'm afraid He wouldn't listen to me," Dick argued, still doubtful.

"But His Word says that He will. He has kept His promise even after all this time. We have so many years ahead of us, if the Lord lets us live. His Word says that 'he that cometh to me I will in no wise cast out.' That means you. Let's pray and you ask God to forgive you and save you and I know that He will. He'll give you the same peace in your heart that I have in mine. That's something that you have denied yourself for so long."

"You pray for me. I can't pray," Dick said, "It's been so long that I've almost forgotten how."

"I'll pray, but you have to do the asking," Brad told him.

"I'll try. You just pray."

Brad began to pray and while he poured out his heart for Dick, that he would realize that God's Word was true, and that he would come to Him and ask for the forgiveness that would bring peace to him after all these years of sorrow and unhappiness. Dick listened silently.

As he prayed, all the bitterness and doubting and rebellion faded from Dick's heart and he broke at last and began to pray as a child would beg a parent to forgive a wrong that had been committed. When the faltering broken words were ended, Dick was weeping like a child. He put his arm around Brad's shoulder and sobbed, "At last I'm free, Ted, free! How wonderful to feel free, that this weight of rebellion and anger and bitterness has been taken away. I've longed so many times for this, but something seemed to hold me back, as if it was something beyond my power to resist and I would be in agony, but I couldn't do anything about it."

"I know," Brad said. "It was Satan. When you first began to doubt God and to harden your heart against Him in bitterness, then you gave Satan the opportunity to step in and harden that heart still more. You had no power to resist him, for you had left God out of your life. How glad I am that you've been delivered from that bondage, even if it took that fire to set you free."

Dick dried his eyes and managed a smile as he nodded in agreement. "I know now that you are right. I could almost feel that oppression and that overwhelming influence every time I felt the urge to ask God for forgiveness."

"There's someone else who'll be glad to know what has happened," Brad remarked. "Nancy will be so glad. She's been praying for you just as I have."

The smile vanished from Dick's face and a sigh escaped him. For the time being, he had forgotten Nancy. Swift pain again darted through him at the mention of her name. At last he had yielded, as she had wanted him to do, but now it was too late. He had lost her. He had no right to grieve now, but he did.

"I hope that you and Nancy will be very happy together," he managed to say, but the mournful tone of his voice belied his words.

Brad stared at him a moment in surprise, then he

laughed. "Did you think that Nancy and I were in love with each other?"

"Yes. Aren't you?" Dick asked, still more surprised. "I thought when I saw you two together so often that you must be."

Light spread over Brad's face. "Now I understand!" he cried, laughing again. "Now I'm beginning to see daylight. Now I see why it was that you seemed to dislike me when I couldn't understand why. You're in love with her, aren't you?"

Dick nodded. "I've been in love with her ever since I first met her. She wouldn't have anything to do with me because I wasn't a Christian. Goodness knows I wanted to be, just to please her, but I couldn't pretend something that I didn't feel and didn't want. How could you keep from falling in love with her?"

"For the very good reason that I'm in love with some-one else. Nancy knew that from the first. Of course because of our interest in the class, we were associated together often and perhaps others also misunderstood. I had a suspicion that she was in love with someone and that perhaps he didn't care for her, for sometimes I would catch an expression of sadness on her face. At the funeral I wondered if it might have been you."

Just then the nurse came in and when she left, while they were waiting for the doctor to give Brad his discharge, he finished dressing.

"Do you know what I've been thinking?" he asked as he was tying his tie. "I've been thinking of that little duel we played with those wooden swords. It's strange that I can remember some things in the past so clearly, yet other happenings I can't remember. I can't remember our mother's face and how I wish I could," and he uttered a sigh.

"Neither can I, though I've tried to so often," Dick told him.

"I remember you started screaming your head off when you jabbed me in the neck because you saw that blood and you thought that you had killed me."

"I sure did," Dick agreed with a faint smile. "I can see you lying there doing a little screaming yourself."

"I thought I was killed," Brad remarked with a little laugh, "but here I am. I've been thinking in what strange ways God sometimes works things out. All the time when I've been trying to hide this ugly scar, it was the one thing that brought us together. If you hadn't poked me with that stick and made this scar, perhaps we never would have known each other even though we were so closely associated here at the plant. Strange, isn't it? But God knew way back there that one day you would see that scar and recognize me. We surely don't have the slightest resemblance. For twins, we're just about as different as twins could be."

"Perhaps you're not my twin, but some foundling that my parents felt sorry for and picked up on the roadside," Dick remarked with a smile. "But it does seem like a miracle that it happened as it did. Now I can thank God for waiting so long to keep His promise." His voice held a new note of reverence. "It's true, what I learned as a little child and had forgotten until now, that God knows the end from the beginning and that He always keeps His Word." He sighed. "How glad I am that I can believe."

"I can say amen to that," Brad added in reverent tones.

When the doctor came, he told Brad that he would find his discharge at the desk. He then examined Dick again and told him that he would discharge him the next day if there were no symptons of any lung damage. Soon after he was gone, Brad prepared to leave.

"I'll see you this afternoon," he told Dick, then, with a wave of his hand and a smile, he was gone.

Chapter Twenty-five

Brad was anxious to see how much damage the fire had done, so he went to the plant at once. Men were already at work on the inside. He learned that most of the damage was on the lower floor where the explosion had occurred, though there was smoke damage on the other floors. Several of the officers of the company were there and they were endeavoring to discover the possible cause of the fire. Two of the fire officials were there also, looking into the possible cause.

Brad went to Dick's office to see what smoke damage had been. He was thankful again that Dick had gone back at the risk of being trapped, to recover those papers that contained such valuable information. It would have taken a long time to work out this information again. The room was damaged by smoke which left its mark upon the open drawer from which Dick had grabbed the papers.

When he saw that he could be of no help at the plant and he knew that it would be days at least before the force could go back to work, he went to his room and cleaned up, then he phoned Nancy.

Nancy told him, when he asked her about the fire, that she had read about it in the morning paper.

"Did you know that Dick James almost lost his life in that fire?" he asked.

"No!" she cried in alarm. "Tell me about it."

He smiled, for he detected a more than friendly interest in her voice. He told her of Dick's rescue just in time, though he didn't mention his own important part in it.

"I believe that it would cheer Dick if you would go to see him this afternoon. I'll pick you up if you would like to go," he offered.

"Oh, thank you! I'd like to go," she told him.

When Brad hung up, he felt like a little boy bursting with a secret that he had to keep. But this secret was something special and he found it difficult to wait until time to pick Nancy up.

Dick had spent the day thinking of the past, trying to remember some of that past childhood when he and Ted were together. He found it difficult to remember much, but as Brad had said, he could remember some things, especially that duel when he had stabbed Ted and had brought the blood.

He remembered what Ted had said about how wonderful it had been, that God had known about that scar and He knew that it would be the means of bringing them together. He was able to remember many of the truths that he had learned from his mother, for he could now think of them in a new light, because all the bitterness and doubt had been taken away.

He prayed again as he thought of all that had transpired, while he thanked God for forgiving him and he asked Him to take charge of his life from now on and to help him to atone as much as was humanly possible for all the wasted years.

Life looked so different now, for he could look forward to happiness, now that he was free to live in the love and peace of this new life. There was only one little dark spot in the view of a cloudless new day, now that he was free from that load of sin and doubt. That little dark spot was the thought of Nancy. He could now go to her with the glad news that at last there was no barrier between them and that they could at least be friends. But he didn't want to be friends. As he had told her that last time they were together, he still felt that it would have to be all or nothing.

He longed to pray that God would let her love him again, for he was sure that her love had long since died, but he felt that he couldn't even pray for that. He didn't deserve her love.

When he had finished his lunch, he drifted off to sleep, for he was still rather weak from his ordeal. He was roused by the sound of voices in the room. When he opened his eyes and saw Brad standing there beside Nancy, he stared at them in surprise.

"I've brought you a visitor, Mr. James," Brad said, then as they drew nearer, he indicated Nancy. "I believe you know Miss Crawford." Before Dick could speak, he turned to Nancy and said, "Miss Crawford, meet my twin brother Tag."

Nancy stared at him a moment speechless, then she stammered, "Your twin brother? I don't understand. You called him Tag. What does this all mean?"

"I'll let him explain," Brad told her with a wink at Dick. "I'll leave you two alone for a while. When you get tired of talking to him, Nancy, you'll find me in the lounge. I'll be waiting there."

He left and Nancy stood looking questioningly at Dick.

"Won't you sit down?" Dick invited.

She obeyed, waiting expectantly.

"It's a long story, but I'll make it as brief as I can," he told her. Then he gave her the main events of his life, his praying that God would let him find his brother and then the wonderful miracle that had brought them together when he was rescued from certain death.

"I couldn't tell you the reason why I was so bitter against God and so reluctant to believe His Word because He had failed me, but I couldn't pretend to believe when I didn't, even to possess your love."

She didn't tell him that his mother had told her some of the story.

"You poor little misguided fellow," she commented when he had finished. "I knew that there was some reason, in the very beginning of our acquaintance, why you were so bitter that you wouldn't even talk to me about God — when I was praying so that you would come to Him and be saved. I still pray, Dick, that you will find peace with God. Now that you have found your brother, why not come to Him and thank Him for letting you find Him? Your brother is such a fine young man," she added.

"As fine as I hope to be some day," he replied.

"But you can never be that unless you come to the Lord and receive His forgiveness for all your past bitterness and doubt," she told him.

He smiled. "I've already done that, Nancy. Didn't Brad tell you?"

"No!" she cried. "Oh Dick, I'm so glad! How I thank God that at last He has answered my prayer for you. I suppose Brad wanted you to tell me. I was beginning to think that maybe God wasn't going to answer my prayers for you, though I knew that He was always concerned about any lost soul."

"Brad is a wise old owl," Dick remarked with a little laugh. "He got a big kick pulling off that dramatic little stunt when he introduced me. I'm so glad that I'll be getting out of here this afternoon, for he and I have to make up for so much lost time."

"I shall rejoice with you," she said.

"I thought you two were in love when I saw you together so often and I almost hated him because of it. But he told me that he was in love with someone else. What a poor misguided fool I was!"

"He told me that he knew you disliked him and he couldn't understand why you did," she told him. "I never dreamed what the cause was, of course, but it seemed to me that you disliked everything and everyone. I was so grieved to see how morose you were getting to be and I longed to be able to say something that would help you.

"The thing that made me most miserable was the knowledge that I had lost your love. I knew that I wasn't worthy of it, but that didn't help me any. I do hope, Nancy, that some day you will find someone who is worthy of your love."

"I don't think that is possible, Dick," she said with a smile.

"What do you mean by that?" he asked.

"I wouldn't even try to look for another such person," she informed him. "I found that person long ago and he almost broke my heart because he would not love my Lord as I loved Him. It was a terrific struggle that I had to face, but the Lord gave me strength to do what I knew He wanted me to do, but not the thing that my heart cried out for."

"Meaning who and what?" he asked while he waited breathless for her answer.

"Meaning someone who once told me that there would never be anyone else in his heart but me. I believe I told that someone that there never would be anyone else in my heart but him. But I think he has forgotten what I said long ago."

"You mean that you still care, Nancy?" Dick asked eagerly.

"How can I answer that unless I know that you still care, unless you tell me that you do?" she asked with a twinkle in her eyes.

"Miss Crawford, I love you with all of my heart, soul, and body," he stated. He reached out and took possession of her hand. "Would you do me the honor of making me the happiest man alive by telling me that you return my ardent affection?"

"Gladly will I tell you that I do return your affection, Mr. James," she said while a little laugh of supreme happiness bubbled from her lips.

"Would you do me the honor of becoming my wife?" he asked, trying to be serious while laughter was rising up within him.

"I would consider it an honor to be your wife," she told him while her eyes shone with new brightness.

"Oh Nancy darling, come here," he commanded while he raised up and held out his arms.

She clung to him while their lips met in a clinging kiss.

"How I have longed for this!" he cried. "I never hoped to have you in my arms again. Oh, may God give us both a long life, for we have so much to make up for."

Just then the doctor entered, followed by Brad.

"It seems that my brother has found a new nurse, Doctor," Brad remarked. "I think she will be able to restore him to complete health much sooner than you expected."

"It seems that she has already done so," the doctor replied as they all laughed, while Dick released the much embarrassed Nancy.

"Don't mind me," the doctor told them. "I'm used to these scenes. I find them more effective than any of the drugs that I prescribe."

Brad, Dick and Nancy drove home together. When Dick reached the house, after bidding the other two good-by, the first thing he did when he opened the door was to kneel just inside and thank God for what He had done for him. Then he went into the rooms which had seemed so desolate and filled with the agony of remembrance. He stood just within the door of each and had a little talk with God. It was amazing to him how easy it was just to talk to God. And how different this empty house now seemed. It held memories that were sacred and he almost felt the presence of the parents he loved as he stood there.

He couldn't sell the house as he had thought he would have to do. It would always hold those sacred memories and he and Nancy would live there as long as life lasted. If they should have children, they would be reared in the atmosphere of love that those who had gone on before had created there. And there would be the hope that at some time in the Lord's plan for the end of this age, they would all be together again, his loved ones and hers.

He stopped at the threshold of the living room and bowed his head.

"Lord, how I thank Thee for the two parents whom You gave me and who made this home such a happy place even while I was so far from Thee. By Thy will, we shall live here and may we live in Thy will always. If we have a family, may we teach them the truth that I now believe, that what Thou hast promised, Thou wilt surely bring to pass."

As he ascended the stairs there was a song on his lips, for tomorrow would be a new day in a new life and he would now dwell in the love and the knowledge of the promise that God had kept. Never again would he doubt.